Originally from Boston, MICKEY J. CORRIGAN hides out in the lush ruins of South Florida to write pulp fiction, literary crime, and psychological thrillers. Her stories have been called "delightful pulp," "oh so compulsive," "dark and gritty," and "bizarre but believable." *Songs of the Maniacs* was published by Salt in 2014.

MICKEY J CORRIGAN

PROJECT XX

A NOVEL OF MOCK SUPERFICIALITY

SALT

LONDON

PUBLISHED BY SALT PUBLISHING 2017

2 4 6 8 10 9 7 5 3 1

First published in Great Britain in 2017 by
Salt Publishing Ltd
International House, 24 Holborn Viaduct, London EC1A 2BN United Kingdom

www.saltpublishing.com

Salt Publishing Limited Reg. No. 5293401

A CIP catalogue record for this book is available from the British Library

ISBN 978 1 78463 097 3 (Paperback edition)
ISBN 978 1 78463 098 0 (Electronic edition)

Typeset in Neacademia by Salt Publishing

Printed and bound in Great Britain by Clays Ltd, St Ives plc

Nick Flynn, excerpt from "AK-47" from *My Feelings*. Copyright © 2015 by Nick Flynn. Reprinted by permission of The Permissions Company, Inc. on behalf of Graywolf Press, Minneapolis, Minnesota, www.graywolfpress.org.

Salt Publishing Limited is committed to responsible forest management. This book is made from Forest Stewardship Council™ certified paper.

"*What I know is my music gets blamed for school shootings.*"
—MARILYN MANSON

"*Sometimes I wonder if I'm a character being
written, or if I'm writing myself.*"
—MARILYN MANSON

& *yes* each of us is born with a gun on the wall *yes* a gun in the
closet *yes* a gun to our heads
—NICK FLYNN, "AK-47"

PROLOGUE

Last Day of Summer Classes, 2012

I T WAS HOT, that was the first thing you would have noticed. And quiet, weird quiet like it is some Sunday mornings in church between songs. Like just after the choir finishes singing and the organ trails off and the notes ease up, soften, drift into mist, then drop away. The classroom smelled like Ivory soap, tropical fruit chewing gum, hazelnut coffee. The room had a lot of people in it but everyone was holding their breath, unmoving, in a kind of religious state of grace. The room itself was between breaths. Hot and still.

H8er stood beside me with the 12-gauge Savage-Springfield 67H pump-action shotgun pointed due east. She looked badass in my rumpled Diesel Lloyd black leather jacket and my mom's high-waist black leggings. I'd loaned her my made-to-order lizard skin cowboy boots with the stacked leather heels and the lemon wood pegs. She was a little wobbly on the Cuban heels, but she stood tall, her pale face serious as ever.

That was the thing about H8er. You could never tell when she was having a good time.

The silver ball stud on her upper lip bounced a little. "You gonna just stand there, pussy?" she said out of the corner of her small, mean mouth. Which was, in a way, kind. Because she didn't want to embarrass me, with us standing up there like on display, in the front of the hushed classroom, everyone staring.

"Don't let's wait for the POPO to get here, *Heidi*," she added. Which wasn't so kind. She knew how much I hated to be called Heidi. Aimee's bad enough.

POPO is what we'd nicknamed the school security team, a couple of buff loser cops who wore tight uniform shorts and boxy tee-shirts stamped front and back with "PO" in black letters. PO for Police Officer. Big whup. All those chrome-domes did all day was ride a couple of crummy blue bicycles around campus, joking about how they were going to frisk the hottest girls.

Not us, though. POPO didn't even see us.

The M1911A1 .45 caliber handgun was slip-sliding about in my sweaty palms. If she'd seen me my mom would have said, "For god's sake, Aimee, stand up straight!" Because I was tipped to the left from the Italian Beretta double-action semi-automatic pistol with 16-round double-stack magazines. Which were weighing down the front pocket of the Army-Navy Surplus fatigue jacket we'd lifted. From my grandfather's closet, along with the guns and a World War II hand grenade that I'd somehow forgotten in the glove compartment of Mom's car.

I was kind of obsessing about what my mother would do if she found it in there. I wanted to write a note to myself to retrieve the grenade ASAP and hide it in my bedroom. Like maybe in the bottom drawer of my AH McIntosh Danish teak breakfront with polished brass handles, under several layers of my J. Crew cashmere sweaters, including the sea-foam green waffle cardigan I'd had no opportunity to wear this past

2

winter. It had been a strangely warm year, we'd gone through a winter that wasn't, one for the record books. Not a single day below sixty degrees. Which is unusual enough for this part of Florida that the local media had worked itself into a total frenzy about hurricane season and global warming and all that pointlessly neurotic stuff.

Yeah yeah yeah, we're all gonna die.

Meantime, H8er and I were creating our own natural disaster this summer. Right here, in the 9 a.m. English Composition 100 class. At Hope Shore's own snobby little institution of higher learning, Hope Shore College.

I was kind of whispering to myself under my breath because I was pretty sure I'd forget about the damn grenade after H8er and I finished shooting up my summer school class. I hadn't been remembering to do what I needed to do since the spring, my mind was just so totally spent. Acid washed. But this was so not the time to get out my notebook and write something down. I had to trust myself, which seemed like a stretch. Trusting my mind was another thing that had been slip-sliding away.

"Dude," I whispered. "You go first. Like, remember: this was *your* idea."

H8er tossed her head once or twice and a little clump of eggshell white bang hair bounced around her broad forehead. She lifted the shotgun and took aim exactly the way we'd been practicing all summer long in the citrus grove west of my house. Her finger tats gleamed with sweat. You would have been impressed by how pro she looked. Like Angelina Jolie in *Salt*.

Before she pulled the trigger, I knew what she was going to say before she said it. "SMD, Aimee."

Suck my dick. Her favorite expression. Mine too. Our favorite thing to say to each other. And the last thing Skitchen Sturter ever said to me.

PART ONE
SPRING, 2012

One: SMD

YOU WANT ME to start at the beginning, though, because then maybe you'll be able to understand how I got from there to here. Where we are now. And you think maybe that will help us see where we might go from here. If there's anywhere left for someone like me to go, that is.

You seem to think there is. Me, I'm not so sure.

So let's get on with it, shall we? Okay, so before I met Skitchen Sturter, aka H8er, I was your typical nerdy girl with your typical nerdy ambitions for college and career. Only in reality, my mom was the one with the ambitions. I was the one with the nerdy looks and nerdy brains, the too smart girl everyone thought would end up going to Harvard or Radcliffe, Vassar or Yale.

It started in preschool, the whole Aimee's headed for an Ivy League college shit. My mom thrived on that big time. For years she was sure it would be Harvard, then she got wind of where the "different" kids go and was all about Brown during my junior and senior years. Me, I didn't really know *what* I wanted. So I studied a lot, like 24/7. I did all the right stuff, marched the expected college-bound goose-step. You know the drill. I brown-nosed and crammed and aced everything I could, volunteering in between, all of that to keep my mom from going ape-shit on me.

If you diagnosed my mom, she would have something like College Mania. Or maybe Neurotic Elitism. She's been like this since I was born, or at least as long as I can remember. Before I even got to my first birthday, she'd launched a college fund at Bank Atlantic in downtown Hope Shore, Florida. When I was a toddler, she pushed me in a stroller around Harvard Yard so she could joke I'd been through Harvard. I shit you not. I got airsick on the plane and threw up a bunch more on the king-size bed at the B&B in downtown Cambridge. The Widener Library was right outside the window. I don't remember any of this, of course, Mom just tells this story a lot. Or she used to, back when she was all psyched up about me going to one of the Ivies.

But you don't want to diagnose my mom. This isn't supposed to be about *her*, is it?

So okay, let's focus on my relationship with Skitchen Sturter. Because you could easily divide my life story into BH and AH: Before H8er and After H8er. That's mostly how I see it anyway. BH, I wouldn't have even *thought* of saying something like "suck my dick." Certainly not out loud, never to anyone's face. But AH, I did stuff like that all the time.

And here we are. Right? *Here we are.*

Mom and I were shopping at the Everglades Mall the first time I laid eyes on Skitchen Sturter. The mall was way crowded. A rainy Saturday afternoon, the beach crowd hanging in the food court, on their phones or throwing french fries. The place reeked of Auntie Anne's Cinnamon Sugar Pretzels and The Body Shop Maca Root Energetic Face Protector.

I tried to walk fast ahead of Mom and pretend I was alone. This was impossible though because she kept calling me back to check out whatever store caught her eye, saying stupid stuff like, "This curvilinear ink stretch dress would look *terrific* on

8

you. It looks like a Stella McCartney Fitzroy, but *without* the cutout!" Or "Look, Aim, Lucky Brand is having a *sale!* Don't you need a *new* pair of Charlie skinny jeans, hon?"

Then Mom spent an interminable amount of time in Brookstone studying a Vinotemp Single Bottle Wine Chiller with CPU controlled temperatures and an insulated sleeve. Just what my semi-alcoholic mother needed: a way to chill her wine faster. My humiliation freaking peaked.

When we were out front, *finally*, on our way to the parking lot, *thank god*, that's when I saw her. Panhandling in the waterlogged courtyard, where a huddle of palm trees dripped rainwater onto splashy rows of multihued annuals. She was by herself. All eyes and bones, with skin the color of flat champagne, she looked like a paint-by-number on velvet. Beggar Girl Under Tree.

She sat cross-legged just beyond the sidewalk, her back against a spiky cabbage palm, a Starbucks cup full of damp dollar bills lodged next to her in the plush grass. Her legs looked stickish, the knees bulging like Tootsie Pops. Her hair was shaved off back then; this was like almost a whole year ago. The nubby bare scalp made her eyes look huge. I almost felt like handing her my shopping bags because all her clothes were major rags. She was strumming a totally beat guitar, sort of singing quietly. Her voice rasped, like she'd already smoked it up pretty bad.

"My god, why doesn't mall security do their job," my mom muttered as we walked past. The air smelled sweet, the smell of freshly smoked la la. The girl looked up quickly, grinned. Her teeth were super white, her eyes a faded blue, her skin see-through pale. She looked washed out. Mom grabbed my elbow and we made a wide berth.

When I glanced over my shoulder, the girl was still looking at us. Laughing. I smiled and raised my eyebrows, like *what can I say, my mom is a pain.* The girl gave me a thumbs-up, then cocked her index finger and pointed it at me. Pulled the imaginary trigger.

In the car, Mom went on a tear about kids with no goals, dropouts and druggies. How awful and pathetic they all are. How drug ed classes like Don't Start with Me are a total waste of taxpayer money. Blahblahblah. I *yessed* her and mainly stared out the window of our Alaska white Land Rover LR2 with burnt almond leather interior and a tinted sunroof. "I'm so grateful I don't have to worry about you, Aimee," she said at one point.

Who was she kidding? All she did was worry about me. Would I make dean's list? How did the biology project go? Was the *Hope Shore Sounder* going to hire me as student editor? How many volunteer hours did I have now at the public library? How did I do at the track meet; did I place? What else could I do to fatten my résumé and make me look well-rounded enough for the top tier college admissions committees?

She neurosed constantly. Coming your way: endless streams of pain-in-the-ass college candidate pressure. It was enough to drive you mad.

"Yeah, that's for sure," I must have said. Or something like that.

Now I'd say, "SMD, Mom." That would give her something to worry about.

But I guess I've done a premier job of that anyway. BH, Mom fretted about me taking college classes senior year, a lot of added work on top of my AP high school courses. She'd asked me stuff like, "Why don't you dual enroll at Hope Shore College senior year? It'll be hard, but the admission office at Brown will *like* that. It shows *initiative* and college readiness." AH, Mom said, "Are you *sure* you're all right? Are you getting *any* sleep *at all?*" AH, I was a total mess. Am a total mess. As you have pointed out repeatedly.

So, as it turns out, Neurotic Mom had reason to be concerned about my future. Maybe she'd had reason to worry all along.

The second time I saw H8er was around six months later. The HuffPo headlines that day were about the failed eradication efforts on Grassy Key down near Key West. The state had declared a premature G.W. Bush-like victory over the Gambian Pouched Rat, an invasive rodent the size of your most overweight house cat. Biologists had lured the critters to poisoned bait for months, later announcing they'd done them all in. Then a year goes by and suddenly residents start seeing the big scary rats again, rummaging in the trash with nasty enthusiasm, nosing across pool decks and scaring babies, ruining people's morning jogs. So wildlife officials had to start all over with the mass murdering. Kill, kill, kill the non-native invader!

Made me want to buy one as a pet and breed it. Or better yet, go down to the Keys and rescue some before they nibbled on globs of peanut butter laced with pesticides. Why are outsiders always being bullied?

I was trolling around on my iPhone, looking for something to relieve my boredom. I was at school early because Mom had to meet a client at eight o'clock and she wanted to prepare at the office first, "get her head on" for her first showing. So she dumped me at the Central High School library at six-thirty. An hour before it even opened. I slumped on a bench made from recycled plastic milk cartons (like *that's* gonna save us from the global environmental crisis) under a sweet-smelling dogwood tree.

Bored with the day's meaningless trivia, I set the HuffPo "news" aside and started reading Yeats. An assignment for my college lit class. Yeats rocks, but reading a bunch of his stuff at once can be dulling, especially first thing in the morning.

So maybe I nodded off a little, like once or twice. The night before I'd had trouble sleeping and I ended up reading until three. Had my nose buried in *Softer than His Voice*, a trashy novel I found on my mom's Mid-Century Nightstand with beveled front edges and antique brass knobs from ZGallerie. What a bunch of duh drivel romance fiction is. Somehow, though, I kept flipping the pages, weirdly rooting for the dewy-eyed goodie-goodie to win over the domineering life-guard with the six-pack abs. If only I'd been that kind of girl. How simple my life could have been! People who know the brand name of everything and the value of nothing have it so much easier in life.

Yeats had it down about that kind of stuff. After I fuzzed through a couple of poems, I kind of scanned the empty campus around me. The night had been a tiny bit cool so there was a foggy mist on the little manmade lake just beyond the flagpole. A couple of snowy egrets swooped in and out of the fog, calling to one another. A loud blue jay fought it out midair with a bitchy crow twice his size until the big black bird gave up and darted away. This made me laugh.

And that's when I spotted her. On a bench on the other

side of the lake, gazing up at the sky, grinning like I was at the battle of the birds.

Suddenly, she looked right at me. Startled, I managed a little wave. She waved back.

Even with her hair grown in, I recognized her right away. The panhandle girl from the mall. She sat cross-legged on the bench, her face hard to read in the mist between us. But when she beckoned me over, I stuffed my copy of *The Collected Poems of W.B. Yeats* in my chili pepper red North Face Recon backpack with FlexVent padded shoulder straps and hip belt (endorsed by the American Chiropractic Association), and followed the narrow asphalt path around the curve of the lake.

She was sitting in the middle of the bench, but as soon as I got there she scooted over to make room for me. Her shorts and tee-shirt looked even rattier than before, if that's possible. The front of her wrinkly shirt had two cartoonish fried eggs and block print that read *Cholesterol: Silent Killer*.

I sat down next to her, dropped my backpack on the ground by my feet. We smiled at one another.

"Go, blue jay, huh? Love it when the little guy beats up on the big bully."

Her voice seethed with smoke and something else, something foreign. Not an accent, but a kind of ironic maturity. I understood that before I knew I did. At the time, I was mesmerized by her strange looks, her unusual blue-white paleness, and her seemingly genuine interest in me.

When I nodded, she said, "Skitchen Sturter. Call me Hater. That's H, the number eight, E, R."

"Aimee Heller," I said.

We stared at one another, sizing each other up. Her angular face was clean, unblemished, but her elbows and knees were scuffed and dirty. Black grime had been ground into her long thin feet and toes, which looked totally gross. But she smelled like spring, floral and fresh. Unless that was the dogwoods. I thought she was pretty in a haunted, I could use a good meal and a pint of blood kind of way.

"Hey, Hater and Heller, that's cool," I said, instantly regretting how duh I sounded.

But she laughed. "Yeah, it *is* cool. Heller's a totally down name. You're lucky there. Had to create a fucking avatar for myself so I didn't have a total fucking meltdown every day from everyone fucking up my name."

I probably looked at her in some pussy way because she laughed at me and leaned over, whispering in my ear, "Fuckafuckafucka, muthafucka." Then she sat back and grinned at whatever expression was on my face. "SMD! Don't tell me you're one of those uptight Christian bitches?"

At the time I sort of was, but I really didn't want to be. The church thing was Mom's trip, one of them anyway. She said belonging to Calvary Chapel and teaching a God Knows Us class to second-graders was good for my résumé. I did enjoy the organ music, but really, the rest of it was an insulting bore. And, when it came right down to it, I don't think Mom bought it either. Like how could anybody not totally laugh at the wigged out idea that abstinence before and between marriages was the way to go? I mean, me and Mom didn't talk about this stuff. But, you know, there was a ton of do as I say, not as I do going on at my house. Plus, Mom spent the whole hour in the back row pew with her head bowed, texting and reading the Sunday edition of USA *Today* on her smart phone. She made *me* sit up front with all the born-agains.

"What's SMD?" I asked H8er, although I knew I should

figure it out for myself. It had to be obvious, like OMG or LOL. But I can be dense sometimes, even with the English language. Which is, I must admit, my one and only real gift.

Yeah yeah yeah, I've been in "gifted" classes. And AP and honors classes, too. Top of the class pretty much my entire school career. And I'm a supposedly "gifted" varsity cross-country distance runner. *Not super-fast, but super long winded*, as Coach Meyer likes to say. But the truth is, most of my accomplishments are just a testament to persistence. I'd say to *my* persistence, but most of it comes from Mom. She's a persistent nag.

Except for the urge to write. The burning desire to write great stuff, that comes from me. I write all the time, and nobody has to push me to do it. Because really, my one true gift is writing. I can tell a story and make you like it. That's an art, and for me it's an obsession as well as a talent. Writing is the one thing in my life I do not want to take a dump on.

"Suck my dick, Heller? SMD? Suck. My. Dick." She poked me with her bony elbow. *Ouch.* "C'mon, get with the program. Where've you been all these years, under a rock?" She was smirking but in a nice way, so I didn't feel too egregiously stupid.

She leaned over, picked up my ridiculously heavy pack from the grass. The canvas was slick from the heavy mist. It smelled like a pup tent. When I looked across the lake, it wasn't so easy to see the bench I'd been sitting on earlier.

"Let's take a look at what you've been up to in Dork School," she said.

I didn't want to explain that half the books in the pack were for my classes at Hope Shore College. Being dual enrolled is totally a nerd thing. H8er already had me pegged as an egghead, I didn't want to feed her any more ammunition.

That would come later.

"Whoa, dog. What hell is this?" she asked, probably rhetorically, pulling out several of my textbooks.

Before you start thinking H8er was just another in a long line of bullies that had been picking on me since I was a fat first-grader or something, stop right there. I am not a school victim. Okay? In fact, although I was not one of the scholarship jock kids, the superrich privateers, the high IQ geeks who fast track it through high school in like a year when they're only twelve, even though I was never top tier in the class of 2012 subjective as hell social ranking, I was not a loser girl either. Not a goth, stoner, skateboard whore, Biggest Loser, or special ed. Not a breezy bobble-head either. I didn't give myself away to boys, I didn't hide in the second floor bathroom and slug Stoli from my leak-proof Green Mountain Coffee Brown Backpacker Thermos with double insulation, although this type of activity did come to pass eventually. But in high school, I was one of the college-bound smart kids, the Presidential Scholar wannabes, the National Honor Society grinds.

Grind Most Likely to Succeed. You know the type. Not popular, but not unpopular either. The rest of the kids at school knew who I was, we talked, it wasn't so bad. But they didn't really give a shit. I had my few friends, and that was it. Fine with me. I didn't give a shit about the rest of *them* either. As long as they didn't try to feed me any poisoned peanut butter, life was good enough.

This is not one of those trite Bullied Kid Gets Revenge stories. You must have seen your share of those already. Me and H8er? We were nothing like that.

"Physics for Doofuses, Advanced Calculus for the Categorically Insane, Macroeconomic Theory for Empiricists. Wow, this shit is like pornography for the one percent. Yeats? Okay, he's cool. But I'd rather fuck him than read him." When she laughed, her mouth didn't shift. I mean, a laughing sound came out but she didn't look happy or anything. "No Plath? No Theory of LGBT Liberation? No feminist lit reader? Why the fuck not?"

I yanked the backpack from her nail-bitten hands and dropped it back on the sodden grass. "How can you play guitar with those chawed up fingernails?" I asked.

"Quit that shit a few weeks back. No money in it. Sold the guitar to some punk in the food court, the best profit I ever got from my music." She hid her hands in her armpits. "But now H8er needs a new gig. Gotta find a way to make some quick bucks. Any ideas, genius girl?"

Was she hitting me up? I shrugged. Maybe I had like five dollars on me. For emergencies, tampons or a bottle of Advil if I needed it.

"Don't get all prissy-bitch-snob on me, Heller. Not asking for a handout, for fuck's sake. Just asking if you know about any paying work I might get around town."

I wanted to tell her nobody would hire her in those horrid clothes, but I simply shrugged again. "Let me think about that. It's hard to get any kind of work right now with the recession and all."

"Hellz yeah. Occupy my ass, Mr. Businessman. But you and your mom have a nice set of very pricey wheels, so maybe there's an income stream flowing to you that I might tap into. Somehow." She did that mouthless laugh again.

I smiled, wondering what the hell she was up to.

Suddenly she leaned toward me and sniffed. "You smell great. Like daffodils and red licorice. Yum. Have any like body spray on you? Can I borrow a squirt, I mean? Haven't had a shower in x days."

X *days* could mean anything. I shook my head. "Not *on* me. You'd have to come over to my house after school."

She stared at me for a few seconds, her faded eyes searching mine. The color of her eyes is not easy to describe. Like moon ring gemstones in pastel shades. First the irises would look more purple than blue, then totally blue, then almost gray. And the color itself was faint, like it had been whitewashed.

"OMG. Like, was that an invitation?" When I didn't say anything, she hollered, "Well, okay Aimee Heller! Par*tay*! After Dork School, your place. Be there."

I wrote my address on a sheet of notebook paper and she pocketed it, grinned at me, mouthed *SMD*. When I smiled, she slid off her side of the bench and walked away. Not toward the school entrance and not toward the library. Off somewhere, off campus. Her gait wasn't hurried, but it seemed purposeful. More purposeful than you'd think for a barefoot homeless person in dumpster dress.

Although I wasn't really sure at that point if H8er was a homeless person. Maybe she just liked to look like a bum and beg money from suckers. That actually seemed like something she'd get kicks from doing. For all I knew, she could have been living with relatives or crashing with friends in one of the beachfront estates along A1A. In Hope Shore, it's difficult to separate the richies from the posers. The wealthy often dress poorly, and you rarely see anyone in a suit and tie. Eccentrics are common and commonly accepted. In case they turn out to be multimillionaires, I guess.

My mom doesn't go for weird people though. She likes them born and bred upper-crust, or at least *nouveau riche*. So I knew she wouldn't be too thrilled to see my filthy new friend lounging around on my daiquiri pink Lilly Pulitzer hundred percent Egyptian cotton La Te Dah bedspread.

If I were to bring that girl home, I'd need a plan. Obviously, I would have to lend H8er some of my clothes.

I sat there thinking about what I could do. First I would get her to take a nice long shower (my bath was recently re-modeled in gorgeous ABK Campaginese Evolution, a darling Italian tile in a real sweet coffee milkshake shade called Café). I'd tell her she could use my Ookisa Fortifying Shampoo with Keravis and the Instant Volumizing Soufflé. That stuff really does wonders for limp hair. And whatever scents H8er liked, she had plenty to pick from. I had several shelves of botanicals, and some super expensive French perfumes I'd borrowed from Mom's vast collection.

The idea of the upcoming makeover excited me. Like H8er was some life-size Barbie doll and I could just go home after school and fix her up. Like I was a nonprofit charity organization and she was the token urchin.

Sometimes I totally disgusted myself.

SMD, Aimee Heller. SMD, *Heidi*.

Two: BFF

I SAT ON the bench smiling to myself as the sun broke through the mist, burning the humidity from the air, drying the tufts of grass by my feet and heating the plastic slats under my butt. I was wearing American Eagle Outfitters white jean cutoffs, my JOIE Nancy Peasant Blouse with three-quarter bishop sleeves, and neon pink flip-flops with Hawaiian floral print from Lord & Taylor.

Some time went by. Maybe a minute, maybe a bunch of them. A green heron waded into the shallow lake to catch a tiny lizard and swallow it whole. I couldn't watch. Nature can be terribly cruel. Overhead, fluffy clouds advanced in formation like a marching band of headless snowmen. It started to get hot.

When I checked the time on my iPhone 4S, it was 7:25. In five minutes I could go into the library and cool off. I was starting to sweat. First, however, I would ask Siri an important question. Yeah yeah yeah, I know "she" is actually voice-activated computer software, I'm not a crazy person. In reality, I was just messing around when I said, "So, Siri, what *is* the meaning of life?"

It took a few seconds to process, then Siri's creepy modulated voice responded, "I cannot answer that right now, but if you don't mind waiting, I'll write a long play with the kind of ending that doesn't make any sense."

Touché. Techno-existential humor. I'd read Sartre, Camus. So I smiled.

My sense of peace in the glittery silence, pockmarked occasionally by the trill of a mocking bird or the gentle slap of palm fronds in a slight breeze, was crapped on suddenly by the steady clomp of wedge heels on asphalt. I didn't rouse myself from my trance, however, until she plopped onto the bench beside me and bumped against my hip.

"Whaddup, Aimee. Like who were you talking to?"

Kiko-Ruth Beckman, otherwise known as Bitsy, my BFF since like first grade. We'd drifted apart senior year, though. Mostly because she'd grabbed herself an early acceptance at Cornell and I was shit, wait listed at three schools, none of them first choice. My mom had warned me not to hang around Bitsy anymore if it depressed me.

She was right, I guess. But *not* hanging around my best friend depressed me, too. And not getting into any of the Ivy League colleges? I wasn't sure how I felt about that. Feelings, feelings; how *did* I feel? Twisted up inside? Enraged, maybe? Suicidal? Homicidal? I didn't know. Time would tell, of course. Time would show me just how angry I was. About everything.

"New friend of mine," I told Bitsy. "She doesn't go to Central. I don't think."

I was pretty sure H8er was not one of us. My high school was big, over a thousand students from five neighboring towns, but I would've known all about her if she'd enrolled. Especially here, in small town America. Where a nose up your ass makes you feel like one of the crowd.

"So, you want to ask Siri something?"

I held out my phone and Bitsy shook her head. Her hair was like a shroud, a sleek mass of long, thick, bootblack hair that hung to her waist. At five-two, Bitsy was mostly hair.

And glasses. She had aviator glasses, big googly things, and mirrored shades like the state troopers wear.

"Are you like avoiding me, Aimee?" She crossed her legs primly. She was wearing a blue and white checked pantsuit from like 1976 or something. Vintage Christenfeld of California. And Prada lace-up suede ankle boots with three and one-half inch heels and crepe soles. I was there when she bought them at Nordstrom. She tucked her Tory Burch handbag from Neiman Marcus between us like a wedge of brown leather cheese. That's Bitsy. Perfect. No wonder Mom loved her.

Until she got valedictorian and I got squat.

"Of course not. I have this paper due tomorrow at HSC, and finals week for me is coming up real fast. I'm taking all my finals early so I can start the summer classes at HSC. So, like nothing personal, Bitsy. It's just there's a lot of pressure right now, okay?"

"Are you sure it's not something else? Besides homework? Like maybe you don't want to hang out with me because you didn't get that scholarship to Duke? I mean, I know that's like where you really wanted to go and all. I feel so bad about it, too. Like it really sucks that you can't blahblahblah . . ."

Ugh. Tune out time. She meant well, of course. Bitsy: number one friend, a hundred percent loyal, always had my back. We'd spent every weekend together for almost four years, hanging out at one another's houses, studying and trying to pump each other up for whatever we had to face. Tests, overdue homework, social events we had to appear at, parties we weren't cool enough to attend, the one prom we did go to (what a farce that was, but at least we could laugh about it together), my track events, her piano recitals, on and on. She was a true BFF.

Too bad I hated her guts.

"No, no. No big deal," I interrupted, trying to shut her up. "I'm still waiting to hear from William and Mary. Mom wants to drive up to Virginia and talk to someone in the admission office? If we do that, my weekend is totally blown. I'll miss Monday classes, too. So I have to get all my work done now, just in case."

When I smiled, it felt like the sun had baked my lips to my teeth.

"So you've decided on William and Mary?" She meant well, but she was so asking for it.

"No, I didn't *decide* on anything. I'm still wait listed everywhere, but William and Mary takes more wait list students than the other two schools. So my chances are better there. Mom wants to go up in person and burst in on the admission committee and like fall to her knees on their Persian carpet and grovel and somehow convince them to let me in. So I haven't decided on anything. Not *me*. *I'm* happy to be allowed to attend Hope Shore College. With all the rest of the local losers."

Actually, I wasn't so sure I didn't mean this. HSC has a lovely campus with bursts of coral pink azaleas all over the lush lawn, thick groves of hundred-foot tall Norwegian pine trees, and rambling Gothic mansions where the classes are held. Most of the courses are low pressure, and the profs tend to be enthusiastic, helpful, and devoted. The school has a lame rep because they let in kids with learning disabilities and rich kids whose parents donate big piles of dough. But I liked it okay there and, in some weird way, it was less stressful than Central. I was sure it would be less stressful than one of the Ivies. Or even William and Mary, where I wasn't wanted.

Maybe I had accepted my lower tier worth. Which was totally sickening. I hated myself for it. Why was I content with so little?

"Don't say that, Aimee. HSC is such a nice school. You like Professor Whitehead, right? And you did well last semester. You're doing great there. Besides, you could always go through freshman year, then transfer to like Duke after that?"

Her perky little face lit up as if she'd actually suggested something brilliant. As if I had a choice, like she did. Cornell or Columbia? Bard or Cornell? Oh dear, oh dear, what's a brilliant Asian-American Jewish princess with 760 SATs and a full ride to Cornell to do?

My own so-called choices were limited to attending the local college or committing suicide. Maybe both? Hey, I had options too! I stood up, retrieving my bulky backpack.

"Sure. Okay, so I need to head in now and hit the books. You coming?"

My lips were like dry toast in my mouth. Bitsy followed me around the lake toward the library. I hurried so she couldn't keep up. My legs are like twice the length of hers. Leaving her in the dust gave me a dizzying degree of twisted up joy.

I left her at the bottom of the steep steps of the library, taking them two at a time while she abandoned any attempt to catch up. Before I pushed through the revolving glass doors, I looked back. She was walking off slowly, headed for the main building.

Around her, the campus was starting to pick up. Kids gathered in cliquey knots, laughing, flirting. Bitsy kept her head bowed. Her hair rustled a little in the light ocean breeze coming from the east. She looked tiny, forlorn.

STBY, *Miss Valedictorian*, I thought. Sucks to be you.

BFF? SMD.

Three: Driving Me Crazy

MOM PICKED ME up that evening after track. My hair was still wet from the shower and my legs felt super heavy. I felt like I was walking on a couple of thick tree stumps. I lifted my tired thighs one at a time with both hands to position myself carefully in the passenger seat of the Land Rover. *Ouch.*

Sighing, I leaned back against the headrest.

"Rough workout today, Heidi?"

She didn't care how much I hated her stupid nickname for me. She'd called me that since before I was able to verbalize a protest. And after I asked her not to? She still called me Heidi.

Exhausted from the masochism of laps and sprints, I was in no mood to argue. Or even talk. So I nodded, closed my eyes.

"Want to get Chinese tonight? I don't feel like cooking. Again." Mom laughed at herself. *Ha ha, I admit it: I'm so not domestic. Isn't that forthright and feminist of me?*

My mother the liberated working gal.

"Take my phone. Call Lotus Garden, it's in my address book. Order whatever you're in the mood for."

I opened my eyes. "What about you?"

She was smirking. "I have a date."

This was nothing new. Mom was hot and in demand. In certain circles. Divorced or looking to get divorced, hard bodied and hard drinking, this-close-to-trashy, those kinds of circles. But Mom looked good, so she didn't have to go too long between boyfriends. She jogged three miles on the beach every weekday morning, and worked out every other day at Le Club in Royal Palms. Which is where she met a good percentage of her dates.

My dad was long gone. I'd been basically single-parented from day one.

"He's a hottie," Mom bragged.

She always said that. In the beginning.

"And he *really* likes me."

She always said that, too.

I had no way of knowing, but somehow I doubted both statements.

She didn't bring her men home very often, thank god. She serial dated, humped and dumped, usually keeping me out of it. Which was thoughtful of her. I really didn't want to wake up on Saturday mornings and have to look at some *guy* across the breakfast table.

Until I asked the expected questions, we drove along in silence. I watched the traffic clot along Federal Highway, shiny SUVs and sleek luxury sedans weaving around us as Mom maneuvered in and out of the clogged lanes. The setting sun was blinding my left eye but I turned toward her and fake smiled. Still, I didn't say anything.

She looked tired. Wisps of red-gold hair drifted from her neat little bun, and her mascara had melted, smudging downward toward her high cheek bones. *Thirty-nine, and this is all you get*, her narrow shoulders seemed to be saying.

Mom was wearing a light gray two-button wool and mohair Armani jacket with wide lapels, an Anne Klein silk Charmeuse Blouse with a hidden button front placket, and her current favorite, seamless black leggings from Saks. She looked sort of ridiculous, but she got away with bizarre mismatched fashion somehow. I guess because her outfits were expensive, so people thought she was chic.

Today she flashed some nice bling. The so cool Philippa Holland Ivy Leaf hair clip that I lusted after, and the drop earrings with lightning bolts by Stefan Patriarchi that she'd allowed me to wear to junior prom. Best thing about prom night was I didn't lose those earrings. Or anything else, if you know what I mean. I wasn't about to give it up to Sean Murphy.

Not that he'd asked for it.

Mom sighed longingly. She so wanted me to show interest. Yawn. But, finally, I gave in. I was just too nice to her. I always gave her what she wanted. If I didn't, I felt guilty. Besides, a few minutes of ass-kissing wouldn't kill me. After all, she'd be gone all night and I would have the whole house to myself. I could afford to toss her a bone.

"Okay, so who is he? How'd you meet him? At Le Club?"

"Nope." She perked up instantly. It was so pathetic I had to close my eyes and press myself into the seat. "This fellow's the real *deal*, Aim. College professor. D-I-V-O-R-C-E-D. Fortynine, gorgeous blond and tan all over, gentlemanly, mature. Intellectual, too."

Yeah, right.

My turn again. "Did you meet him at Stars and Scythes?"

Mom's favorite pickup bar. A hangout for middle-aged horndogs.

"Yup. Right you are. Remember last Thursday when I went out with that guy from work, the one I told you wore too many pinky rings? Joey?"

I nod, wishing I could turn on the radio and listen to

NPR. But she'd really flip if I did that. Mom hates it when I'm not listening to every single word of her boring, predictable stories.

"Well, me and Joey were sitting at the bar and it was *super* crowded. But somehow, it must have been *fate*, I spotted this guy Marc. His name is Marcus so it's Marc with a c. And he was watching me from across the room, staring like *mad*, just *waiting* for his chance to come talk to me!"

She was piteously excited. Like this was the first time ever that some jerk had picked her up in a bar.

"So I gave him the eye and excused myself to go to the ladies. Marc followed me and waited outside. I *knew* he was out there, I just knew it. But I came out and acted all surprised. We talked for a few minutes, he put my number in his cell. Today, just as I was leaving the office to come get you, *he called!*"

I wanted to tell her he was married. Obviously. Otherwise, why would he wait until the last minute to ask her out? Because he'd had to wait until he was sure he could get out of the house. He'd waited to make sure the coast to her bed was clear of spouses. Obviously. They all did that.

Well, I wasn't about to pop Mom's happiness balloon. She would just have to find out the hard way. Again.

My turn.

"So where's he taking you?" *Or are you gonna end up paying for him when he realizes he's "forgotten" his wallet? So there'll be no credit card trail for his wife to find?*

Why was I the one who knew all this in advance? Maybe because I'd been paying attention through the last dozen or so boyfriends.

"I'm supposed to meet him at 9," Her voice was practically

oozing joy. It was nauseating. "At an *exclusive* little Italian bistro. In *Boca!*"

OMG, Boca Raton? Could the restaurant be any farther away from Hope Shore? Of course, they wouldn't run into any friends of Professor M-A-R-R-I-E-D twenty miles south, hidden in some dark corner, deep in the Jewish Riviera. Mom was hopelessly doomed with this one already. Why couldn't she see that?

"I *love* Boca," she said. "Whenever I'm down there I notice the *best* results in plastic surgery. It's incredible. It's like nobody's wearing their original *flesh* anymore. Those people are risk takers. I find it . . . inspiring."

She wasn't kidding. That's what's so scary about Mom. Her sincerity.

We stopped suddenly and I opened my eyes, hoping to see the unguarded security booth at the entrance to Palm Ridge Hills. Whoever heard of guard booths with nobody in them? What was the point? They looked good to the snobs and criminals, I guess. All the developments in Hope Shore had them. Except for the mega-homes with real security guards. With semi-automatic pistols and bulletproof tinted-glass kiosks.

But alas, we were stopped at the traffic lights on Ocean Boulevard and Palmetto. A few miles left to go before we reached our development. Which has, by the way, many palm trees but absolutely no ridges. And no hills. No super richies either. Just a lot of upper middle-class n'er-do-wells like us.

Mom gunned it just as the light changed. She'd kill me twice if I did that. Mom's driving was for shit. I couldn't wait to get my license so I didn't have to be kiddie carpooled to both my schools. I already knew how to drive. I wasn't bad at it either. But Mom was making me wait to get my license until I turned eighteen. That's what the other moms at her office advised her to do. She was very susceptible to peer pressure.

Sighing as deeply as possible to indicate how much I did not want to know but was asking anyway, I said, "Soooooo, what does he teach?"

She turned to me, her auburn brows arched like up-side-down smiles. She'd plucked them too much, making her look perpetually shocked. "You're gonna *love* this, Heidi. Marcus teaches Creative Writing! At HSC!"

I gagged. Fortunately, I hadn't eaten anything since lunch. Because I would have bolted it all over Mom's almond leather interior.

"Are you all *right*, baby?"

My eyes teared up and I coughed for like a minute. OMG, Mom was going out with Professor Dimitri? *Shit*. What was her goddam *problem*?

The blood rushed to my head and my calves hurt. I leaned forward, coughing. When she reached over and tried to smooth my hair, I shrugged off her hand and pulled away, leaning against the car door. Why me? Why did *my* stupid slut mom have to pick up a department head at *my* stupid hometown college? And why did it have to be *my* freaking department head?

SMD, Mom!

Of course, I didn't say any of this at the time. But I sure thought it. Because it was already AH. And I was beginning to feel something dark and angry. A deep feeling of resentment. Although I didn't really know that yet.

"Are you *okay*, honey?"

She kept giving me the eye, like she wanted me to reassure

her I would be totally fine while she drove down to Boca to give my future college advisor a blow job.

Watch the road, Mom, I wanted to yell at the top of my lungs. Instead, I got control over my gag attack. "Fine, fine. I'm just kinda beat. From track. And I have a ton of homework. I think I'll skip the Chinese tonight. Maybe heat up a pizza later."

Her mood changed when I mentioned the homework. She got all teary eyed and said in this sickeningly sweet voice, "I'm *so sorry* we can't drive up to Virginia this weekend. I so want to confront those *assholes*. How could they wait list *you*, after all the work you've done these past four, no, *twelve* years? Oh, honey. I'm *sure* we can get them to take you. How-bout if we plan to go up there *next* weekend?"

I didn't want to go to Virginia with her *ever*. Please, no, spare me the embarrassment of walking around a college campus with my freaking mom! Besides, the whole thing was hopeless, William and Mary would never admit me. I just didn't make the cut. There, or at any of the other top schools Mom made me apply to. I should have ignored her blind optimism and applied to FSU or UF, Florida's better safety schools. But Mom said no way. She'd been so sure I'd get into Brown. *So* sure.

And now I was doomed to attend Retard U. *Doomed.*

But I didn't let on. I just nodded and faked a smile. Then I reasoned with myself as we approached our development. This could be okay, this thing she had with my future professor. In fact, it could work out. Knowing my mom, she'd be distracted, all emotionally tied up with her new man, at least for a while. So it would be easier to talk her out of road trips now that Professor Dimitri was in the picture. With luck, we wouldn't have to go out of state to humiliate ourselves after all. We could stay right here in Hope Shore and do that.

Weirdly, this thought cheered me up, and by the time we pulled into the crushed shell driveway in front of our four car garage, I actually felt pretty good.

Considering.

Four: Dollar Menu

MOM WAS GONE by 8:30. Predictably, she was meeting her date at the restaurant down in Boca. None of Mom's men picked her up at the house. This spared me the awkward discomfort of having to meet and greet as she made her way through icky man after man, but it made me feel sorry for her. Didn't Mom deserve a little respect?

Maybe not. If past history was any indication.

A few words about my dad. Rich. Alcoholic. Married. To somebody else when he and Mom were *an item*, as she likes to call it. Dads is very well-known in certain circles (not my mom's). The man is very private, keeps to himself, but he still sends a very fat check every month. Every month until I'm eighteen, I guess. Or maybe twenty-one, I'm not really sure. He also invested money for me and Mom in some fledgling tech firms and our stocks have done well, very well.

Dads is a *very* kind of guy.

I don't hate him. I could but I don't even know him. Mom calls him "Uncle Moneybags," but she's just as happy to deposit his checks and never see him. That's fine with me, too. I have nothing to say to the man except maybe thanks for the healthy seed, the good genes (I never needed orthodontics and my spine is straight), and the steady supply of cash.

After completing a decent draft for a five-page paper on Yeats' "The Wind among the Reeds," I checked the HuffPo headlines. I'm addicted to the HuffPo headlines. Not for news but for guidance. HuffPo as psychic counselor. HuffPo as life coach. Lots of times I can find a headline that gives me a kind of spiritual totem, a deep philosophical lesson, a bit of essential wisdom. Or a fortune cookie prophecy. For me, the HuffPo headlines are like opening up a Bible and reading a passage.

Like this one: *Woman Offers Sex for Dollar-Menu Cheeseburgers.*

Whoa. Move over trailer trash. What struck me was how my mom's like a Girl Scout troop leader or something in comparison to some. Which cheered me.

I turned off my MacBook Air Notebook with Intel Core i5 and i7 processors and a backlit keyboard, and meandered downstairs to the kitchen. The freezer of our Jenn Air built-in stainless steel refrigerator was full of leftovers from Paisley's, the closest decent restaurant to our house. I selected a foil-wrapped take-out container at random and popped the mystery item into the Jenn Air built-in microwave oven with Speed-Cook. After thirty seconds, the kitchen smelled a lot like shrimp with garlic and roasted peppers. Fine with me.

I stood with my head in the fridge and scanned the drink choices. Diet Pepsi, Pepsi Next, Diet Dr. Pepper, Diet Coke, Coke Zero. Looking at these shelves, you wouldn't guess my Mom weighs like about what she weighed in high school. Or that I tend toward underweight on those National Health Statistics charts the pediatrician waves at me when I get my annual physical for track. I actually think me and Mom are sugar substitute addicts. It happens, you can get addicted to artificial sweeteners. They screw with your brain chemicals. I read an article about it on HuffPo.

When the doorbell rang I had just popped open a can of Coke Zero, so I took it with me to the foyer. On weekends,

Bitsy's mom lets her use their LeMans Blue BMW 328i convertible with an iPod adapter. For most of the last year, Bitsy would just come over like whenever. But she hadn't dropped by for a few weeks. Because I was being a bitch. So I was surprised at how happy I was to see her.

When I swung open our wrought iron custom-made front door with frosted glass panels, I must have had a big dumb grin on my face.

But it wasn't Kiko-Ruth Beckman standing outside my house under the orangey light of a bloated, low-hung moon. If it *had* been Bitsy, you and I might not have anything to discuss. Probably I wouldn't even be writing this stuff down for you. There would be no need. I would be just another college student, a kid who was amassing humongous unpayable loans while absorbing precious little that would ever prove to be of practical value in the real world. I'd be writing useless college papers and bad poetry, attempting to stay alert and interested while my life carried me forward. To whatever. To just another normal life.

But that's not how it rolled. Because Bitsy wasn't at the door that night.

When I yanked it open, there she was. Skitchen Sturter. She stood there with one grubby hand on a side-slung hip. Sheet white and twig limbed, waiting impatiently out on the flagstone stoop. Half-grinning, staring at me, daring me to invite her in.

We looked at one another for a few seconds. Her skin was a blue-cheese blue in the eerie moonlight.

"SMD, if it isn't my new BFF H8er," I said.

"Fuck off, Aimee," she mumbled and pushed her way past me.

36

I closed the door.

Pausing, hand on bony hip, she glanced around the front hall. "I'm hungry, Heller. Thirsty. Pissy. And bored." She looked directly into my eyes. We were the same height but I outweighed her by a significant amount. Her eyes were a soft lavender tonight, the circles around them charcoal. "It's Friday night, Heller. I'm seventeen, and it's muthafuckin' Friday night."

I handed her the Zero and watched her chug-a-lug. She let out a ripper of a burp and we both laughed.

"I smell seafood casserole," she said.

"Want some?"

"Does the pope shit on innocent little Catholic kids?" She was smiling, so I let her remark go and she followed me into the kitchen. Her humor was off, in total bad taste and politically majorly incorrect. One of her many sociopathic traits, as I was to discover.

"Wow. This place is like a fucking castle. How many spics does it take to fill a McMansion?" She paused. I didn't really care to know, but she continued, "None, the spics stay outside and work the lawn."

Whoa, lame. "Duh. Maybe you should shut up and eat something," I said.

She had on super skimpy denim shorts, crusty with what looked like mud and paint splatters, and a baggy tee-shirt with tomato sauce stains down the front. *Think Like a 7 Year Old* was printed in kiddie scrawl above a stick figure drawing of a boy with a cowboy hat shooting a rifle.

I had a zillion questions but I didn't want to be uncool. So I said, "We have this place to ourselves tonight."

She nodded, looking around the kitchen. It's cavernous,

there's a lot to take in. Mom's big on stainless steel, souped-up appliances, glass-front cabinetry full of high-end dishware, and hanging copper pots. You can just imagine. Rachel Ray goes high-end suburban.

The shrimp mixture was steaming so I dumped it onto a MacKenzie-Childs black and white check enamel dinner plate, and took a seat at the Nantucket white distressed hardwood kitchen island with black granite inlay. H8er pulled up a black Bertoia bar stool and started shoveling in the food. She ate like it was her first meal of the day.

Maybe it was.

I used the remote to turn on the stereo. *Just Whitney*. One of Mom's fave albums.

Like two minutes later, when my guest was sucking the last grains of yellow rice from her teeth, I broke the silence. "Want something else? We have more leftovers in the freezer, although I'm not sure what."

She nodded, licking her greasy lips, which glistened with olive oil. I jumped up to zap another mystery dish from Paisley's.

"Who lives here with you?" she asked.

"Just me and my mom. She's out on a date. With a professor from my college."

"Oh, that's nice, Aimee. Is she fucking him?"

I didn't say anything but I checked the Classic Black Kit-Cat Wall Clock with the eyes and tail that move, an art deco piece from the 1930s: 11:30. Yes, Skitchen, my mom probably *was* fucking Professor Dimitri right about now. In his car, parked under the saucy moon, somewhere remote. Maybe in an alcove along A1A, facing the ocean. Or maybe in a parking lot in town behind a strip mall. Or, if he *really* liked her, the way some of them did for a month or two, in a motel.

If she'd hit the jackpot? She was giving him head right now in a fancy hotel suite overlooking the water. Could happen. *Had* happened.

"Whatever," I said, tapping the settings on the microwave. "He's actually fairly attractive, if you like your men boozy and over forty. Like my mom seems to."

"I like my men on a plate. Naked, on a paper plate," H8er said with a sneer.

"So you're seeing someone?" I ventured.

"I don't *see* men. I fuck them, then leave."

She was still sneering. I wasn't sure if she was kidding. You could never be sure with H8er.

She sniffed the air. "Smells like leftover Cuban to me," she said.

While I scooped the steaming *arroz con pollo* onto her plate, she rummaged around in the fridge. Her butt was small, rounded. Her shorts had a lot of holes in them, and I wasn't sure she was wearing underwear. I looked away.

"Hellz yeah," she said, turning to give me a big grin while hoisting a bottle of Baron De Ley Reserva 2006 Rioja. "Now we're talking H8er language."

The bottle of Spanish red had already been opened, so I grabbed a couple of MacKenzie-Childs hand-blown wine glasses with black and white stripes. Mom would kill me twice over for using her good wine glasses. They were hand painted and couldn't go in the dishwasher. I'd have to wash them by hand before she got home.

There was plenty of time for that.

"Par*tay*, Heller," H8er said and I giggled.

No biggie, us having a little vino. Mom allowed me to taste her wine at dinner whenever I asked for a sip. She said it was part of my education, to know my wines. Like the difference between a ten dollar California Chardonnay and a seventy-five dollar bottle of Bordeaux. Nobody wants to be stupid about wine.

H8er pulled out the cork and sniffed it. "I like a nice floral bouquet," she joked.

I let her pour, which maybe was a mistake. She filled both our glasses right up to the top of their specially designed Gold Lustre edges. I couldn't even lift mine or I would've spilled it all over the Teragren eco-friendly bamboo flooring.

Mom was picky about the bamboo. It stained, and high heels could leave crappy little dents. Dogs and cats did damage to soft wood flooring with their nails. Which was part of why we didn't have any pets.

The other reason was Mom is a control freak. Which, after sucking enough wine from my glass so I could lift it without swamping, I tried to explain to H8er.

"Look, you can stay here tonight if you want. But you need to take a shower and borrow some of my clothes. Because if my mom sees you like this, she'll freak. I mean, she *hates* bare feet. *Dirty* bare feet. So she'll make me tell you to leave. She's neurotic about the floors. And stuff."

"What stuff?"

H8er ate the second rice dish in about four bites. I picked out another foil wrapped package and stuck it in the microwave.

"Everything stuff. Dirt, lice, bugs, chemicals in foods, germs, viruses, food borne illnesses, fast food, nuclear energy, SAT scores, college apps, seat belts and airbags, career options for teenagers, gateway drugs, STDs, sexual predators, Twitter. She's maximum uptight. She worries about me."

"What's there to worry about? You're little miss perfect, aren't you?"

I shrugged. "Pretty much. I don't get into trouble, if that's what you mean. My mom has enough to deal with."

We were listening to another one of Mom's CDs. *Bad* by Michael Jackson.

H8er poured more wine. I covered my glass with my hand but she dribbled wine onto my fingers until I laughed and gave in. She filled my glass to the brim again. I sucked my fingers, then carefully wiped up the spill with a MacKenzie-Childs black and white striped linen-cotton blend napkin. We slid our full glasses together and clinked, laughing. I bent over mine and sucked a bunch into my mouth. The rioja was a nice, fruity wine. I liked it.

"Your *mom* has problems? Like what? Guys she's fucking? Who just happen to be *your* professors?"

"No." This sort of pissed me off. Mom's dates were her business, not H8er's. Who was she to give a shit? "Forget I told you that, will you? What I mean is Mom's had to do everything herself. *Alone*. Like be a working mom. Bread winner. Parent. Plus, she's had to help me a lot. Like to get into college and all that. Driving me to school and my volunteer job, track meets, et cetera. Helping with my homework when I was younger, giving me advice and stuff. You know, being a single mom."

"Her being a single mom is not your problem, Heller. Your problem is you being a nerdy drag."

I would have protested but I couldn't. Not really. She was right. I had to agree with her. I *was* a total bore. Basically, all I did was study. And do whatever my mom said. And whatever she suggested in order to make my résumé look good to the college admission departments. That was my whole life BH. And just look where being a good girl and a good student got me: home on a Friday night? Sitting in my room alone, writing a paper for a class at Hope Shore College? Where, if the shit stars continued to be lined up in a shit sky, I'd be matriculating in the fall? Please.

"Your Mom a snow turkey?" H8er asked.

"What's that?"

"White woman who like blacks. The Motown music, it's hers, right?"

I pointed to the archway that led to the living room and said, "Go ahead and put on anything you like."

She sauntered out of the room. Her hips swayed when she walked, and she had a pretty cute butt. Even if she looked twenty pounds too light for her frame.

"Whitney was never on Motown," I yelled.

I don't know where she got the Marilyn Manson album. She must have brought it with her.

"*Born Villain*," she announced when she returned to the kitchen. "And I hate you more than life itself."

I wasn't a Manson fan, but I recognized the lyrics. Not my type of music. At the time, I really didn't have any tastes in music. None that were my own. I just listened to whatever Mom or Bitsy or anyone else had on.

"Cool," I said.

"You ever lift anything?' she asked, sliding onto the stool beside me and leaning across the counter. I baby-sipped my wine.

"Lift?"

"Wow. You speakee English, laydee? Yeah, *lift*. As in, steal. *Take*. You know?"

"No, not really. Except from my mom. Sometimes I borrow her stuff. Without like her permission."

"That's not lifting. I'm talking about doing it up. Boosting. B & E-ing. Like, you ever have any real fun? Ever?"

Acting like a juvie was not my idea of fun. I shrugged. "I study a lot," I said. Like the nerd I am. Or was, at the time.

"What about bars? Clubs? You ever go to a nightclub, little miss Ivy League?"

She drank her wine. She wasn't expecting an answer. She had me all figured out. Meanwhile, I knew nothing about her.

"Where are you staying anyway?" I asked. "Do you live in Hope Shore? Or are you like visiting somebody or what?"

She said nothing. H8er was good at saying nothing if she felt like it. She liked to talk, just not about herself.

"What about *your* mom?" I said after a minute. "Is *she* a snow turkey?"

We sat there, staring at one another. One of her eyes twitched. She had smudges of what looked like dirt in her white-blonde hair. I wanted her to take a shower and clean up. I could picture her in one of my electric blue organic cotton tees and a jean miniskirt. She'd look awesome.

Her eyes darted around the room. "So where's the fucking wine cellar in this place?" Her glass, and the bottle, were empty. "Me want more wine."

I didn't dare tell her that my mom locked up all the un-opened bottles in a climate controlled wine closet in the master bedroom, so I changed the subject.

"Let's go to my room and you can check out my closet. You can borrow anything you want. Take your pick. I have a whole bedroom we had redesigned as a walk-in and it's like filled with great stuff from Lilly Pulitzer, Banana Republic,

L&T. You can borrow anything of mine, I don't care. Except for like two things that I can't lend anyone."

"Whatever I wear of yours will be returned in terrible condition, Heller. *You* will be returned in terrible condition."

I giggled. "How long can you stay? Can you spend the weekend? I mean, do you have to go home or anywhere?"

Not that I wanted her to stay for the weekend. I just wanted to know her plans. And if they would be my plans too.

"Have to fuck a man tomorrow night. Tomorrow is muthafuckin' Saturday night, Heller! So yes, please, I *would* like to borrow your shower and closet. That would be fucking groovy. But first, we need more alcohol."

I sure didn't. I slid my glass toward her, sloshing a little. She nodded her thanks and drank down the rest of my wine. In one gulp. Mom would be appalled. That stuff was expensive. Sipping was the proper speed, not slugging.

"Did you drive here? I mean, where are you gonna meet this man? How old is he? Is he a boy, I mean a teenager, or like an older guy? How are you going to get there?"

Questions were running all over the place in my head, and slurring heavily on the way out of my mouth. It was embarrassing.

"Heller. Calm down. I'm not going to jilt you. We are going to meet this guy, this *man*, not boy. Tomorrow night. We'll be taking the Land Rover. With any luck, we will be sucking cock by this time tomorrow night."

I snorted. Maybe I blushed too because she scowled at me. "You really ought to do something about that prissy thing you've got going. You'll never get decently fucked until you do."

I think I laughed. I remember laughing a lot that night. I

remember another open bottle of my mom's wine being taken from the refrigerator, and I'm pretty sure I remember saying, "There's an astounding number of lost souls in this city."

I remember H8er saying, "Oh, to me my mother's care, the house where I was safe and warm." Or something like that. I don't recall laughing at that, though. Yeats is not funny.

The Marilyn Manson album played at least six times.

At one point, when I slid off the white Bertoia bar stool, my thighs felt totally numb. I started laughing my head off and, for no reason at all, sank to the floor. Then I lay flat on the bamboo and began stroking the polished wood. Like a cat. I swear to god, the floor purred.

My first time ever being this drunk. The most high I'd been before was mildly tipsy.

The last thing I remember H8er saying that night was, "Suit yourself, Heller, but I'm gonna have another drink."

When I tried to stand up and follow her into my mother's room where the wine closet was, I was limp as an Asian noodle. I lay on the kitchen floor in a puddle of feeling. I remember kissing the bamboo. I think it kissed me back.

The morning sun smacked me on the right side of my face. My eyes were glued shut, my mouth ashen, like a book of spent matches. I could taste cardboard, but I think it was just my tongue. I sat up real slowly, then dragged myself across the floor to a shady corner, lay down again and passed out.

Later, the cruel sun hit me over and over, slapping my face until I woke up. I was dizzy, hot, sick to my stomach. I sat up and examined the damage. There were some pretty ugly wine stains on my University Yellow RLX Infinity Tank top by

45

Ralph Lauren, and on one of my mom's striped linen napkins that had somehow ended up wadded in my fist. A couple spots of red on the bamboo too, but I spit on the napkin and rubbed them and they mopped up pretty easy.

I got to my feet and looked around. Two dead soldiers: the rioja and a bottle of shiraz, the Australian Syrah Mom loves. *Like oh shit!* Plus a couple of dirty plates, glasses. No breakage, thank god.

After cleaning up the kitchen and trying not to puke, I hunted for H8er, but I knew it was fruitless. She must have been disappointed and totally bored by the drunken coma I'd slipped into. I knew she was long gone. Mom wasn't home either or I'd already have been knee deep in her shit. I held my head in my hands like it was a leaky coconut while I wandered around the house.

Mom's bedroom door was open, the wine closet locked. It looked untouched. So did Mom's bed, her turquoise Yves Delorme sheets and duvet pulled tight and smooth. Obviously, Mom had gotten lucky and scored an all-nighter. Again.

Lucky me, too.

Up in my room, the Mac was on. My Casablanca hand-designed closet doors were closed. A piece of lined notebook paper had been taped to the louvered slats. In red felt-tip marker: "Houston, we have a drinking problem. YOU cain't hode your likker. Like OMG! We need to work on that, dude."

I opened the closet and began rustling through my clothes. *Shit.* My new Lily White Trim Tunic with the green elm tree pattern was missing. *SMD, H8er!*

Leave it to her. She would have to pick my fave shirt.

After that painful discovery, I didn't feel like searching

46

around to find out if anything else was missing. I wrote a note to myself and posted it on the desktop of my laptop: *Get Tunic back from H8er!!!*

I stretched out on the floor and closed my eyes. My head was splitting. So much for red wine. I would have to switch to beer.

At least that was the plan.

Five: SNL

S HE DIDN'T COME back on Saturday night, which was both good and bad. Good because I felt like warmed up dog-doo and didn't want company; bad because I was worried she'd given up on me. Me, complete loser girl, terminally nerdy, fatally uncool. But, as it turns out, H8er would hang in there with this nerd girl. In fact, she had big plans for me. For us. Just not for that particular weekend.

I lay flat on my bed with a damp Authentic Hotel and Spa one hundred percent organic Turkish facecloth (in cinnamon; I had a set in coral too) over my eyes when Mom got home late Saturday afternoon. She said, "Oh Heidi. Not another *migraine?*" And she took the facecloth into my bathroom to soak it with hot water. When it was steamy, she wrung it out and carried it back to my bedside.

"Thanks, Mom," I said. Weakly. I had a headache but not a serious one. Still, I let her tend to me like she did when I was truly immobilized. I even groaned a little when I reached for the cloth. I didn't have a migraine, though, which I sometimes get and which are teeth-grindingly painful. What I had was a hangover. A red wine hangover.

I smiled at Mom. Weakly, of course. But she looked like she had a pretty good hangover too. Her hair was down and all mussed, unbrushed, her eye makeup mostly rubbed off. Dark circles made her eyes look extra bugged. After we exchanged glances, she popped her Roberto Cavalli retro sunglasses back on her face.

As I repositioned the hot washcloth over my eyes, I heard her sink into my Pebble faux leather wing chair with hand-applied bronze nail heads from ZGallery. She was waiting for me to ask how her "date" went. But I absolutely did not want to hear a single salacious detail about the night she'd just spent with my future professor. My nausea would return. I might upchuck into my own mouth and choke to death. Or something.

The silence in my bedroom pulsated with her desire. The desire to *share*. Mom absolutely *had* to share her feelings. About everything. It was torturous. Which was why all her men eventually fled. Men hate to have to be on the receiving end of streaming emotions and play-by-play relationship analysis. Even I know this. Guys are bored with women who spew reams of romantic data in terminally boring detail.

I hated it too.

She sighed a couple times, shifted on the sticky seat, her nylons shushing as she crossed or uncrossed her legs. I squeezed my eyes hard, feeling the warmth of the towel soak into my skull. A blue jay trilled outside the open window. I would have enjoyed the caress of the light spring breeze which was rustling across my bare arms and legs, but I was trying too hard to ignore Mom by keeping quiet and still. Like I was that weak.

Of course, eventually I gave in. I always did. I'd learned at a young age that the easiest way to make her go away was to let her talk herself out. Then she'd leave me alone for a while. Or drop the subject at hand. Which was, at that moment, Professor Marcus Dimitri.

When I pulled off the washcloth, she was staring at me. I could feel her anxiety or excitement like the pounding of a drum solo in my head. Unless that was my hangover revving up. Whatever it was, it throbbed in the dim light between us. I sighed.

I give. Go ahead, Mom, spill it.

"So, how was your date?" I held the cloth in one hand while I sat up, propping myself against six or seven multihued Etro Fringe Italian satin pillows. From Saks. "Did he fall in love with you yet?"

A little joke we had. Every man fell in love with her at first. Until they ran for the hills. *My pattern*, Mom called it. She'd worked on it in therapy.

"Oh, Aim. He's *terrific*! Cultured, smart, a real *gentleman*. We had *such* a romantic evening. I could fall for this guy, I really could."

I'd heard that before.

"Details," I said.

I get points for saying details. It may be Mom's absolute fave word. Only when she's telling the stories, though.

"The place was *divine*. One of those out of the way European places. And it was nearly empty by the time we sat down. We did have a drink at the bar first, which was all polished wood and brass, very cozy. Oh Aim, it was *so* romantic. And the waiters were *totally* discreet, it was *perfect*. White linen, nice crystal, three-piece jazz trio. I mean, we're talking real class, Aim. And Marc really knows his wines. You know how much I appreciate *that* in a man."

Wine. Oh please, please don't tell me about the wine!

It had taken me like an hour to find the key to her wine cabinet. Deep in her panty drawer, under the twelve-inch

Victoria's Secret pile. Next to a tempting wad of rolled up twenties. Remind me to always look there first from now on.

Transferring two bottles to the kitchen, I replaced the wine we'd drunk (and I do mean *drunk*) with similar ones from her locked stash. I was crossing my fingers, hoping she wouldn't notice they were not the same vintage as the ones we'd polished off. I had to open both bottles and pour some down the kitchen sink, just to make it look right. I totally gagged at the smell. In fact, I threw up in my mouth. Then in the sink. Ugh. I didn't want to think about it.

"Well, long story short, we both had maybe a *little* too much to drink. So Marc didn't want either of us to drive back. *Especially* on I-95. He says the South Florida cops run a bonus pool, they have a ticket quota, with so many drunk driving arrests required per week or something. So we stayed over at his apartment. In Delray." She took off her shades and rubbed her eyes. "The man has *taste*. Really cute little place, with a balcony. Nice ocean view."

"He lives in Delray? I thought he taught at HSC? He commutes all that way every day?"

My skepticism lurked beneath the surface but she didn't catch on. Most of the time, she just didn't.

"No, silly." She snorted. Even her voice sounded hungover. An octave lower, devoid of spirit. I knew how that felt in my own throat. "He lives *here* and rents a condo on the ocean down *there*. So he can spend time away from everything. And do his *writing*. Marc is a *novelist*."

Duh. What creative writing prof didn't consider himself a novelist? Even though most of them couldn't publish their works of genius. Because they were, in reality, crap writers.

Just to be mean, I said, "Oh? Has he written any best-sellers? Anything I might have heard of?"

She frowned, looked puzzled. Not sure if I was goofing on her.

"Here, let me take that." She came and got the facecloth, carried it into the bathroom. "More hot water?" she called.

"No, thanks. I've been working on this all afternoon. I think it's as good as it's gonna get. Until I sleep it off."

She came back in the room, drying her hands on one of my cinnamon hand towels. "Speaking of sleeping it off, I'm up for renting a dumb movie tonight and passing out on the couch. What do you say? How-bout *Pretty Woman* again? You up for that?"

So much for me and H8er using the Land Rover. Our only chance at ever taking Mom's car would be if she went out with friends some night (possible) or if a guy picked her up for a date (like I told you, not gonna happen). But I sure didn't want to go have weird sex with some grown man like H8er had talked about us doing, so the transportation conflict was actually a relief. An excuse that maybe wouldn't make me sound too prissy. If H8er showed up in my Lily White shirt, demanding that we head off somewhere in the Land Rover.

Which she didn't.

"Sure, Moms," I said from my bed. "Sounds perfect."

The HuffPo headline that caught my eye that night was Vegas Doctor Vows to Cure Your Hangover in One Hour, so I read the whole article. Amazing. In Las Vegas, a physician will come to your hotel room and set up an IV to pump you with vitamins and anti-inflammatories and stuff until you feel well enough to go back to gambling and drinking again. It costs, but the article said that, in the long run, you don't lose a whole day lying around feeling terrible. You could count that as saving money, right? That idea has brilliant marketing potential. It could go global, easy.

Mom and I snoozed together on the Do Lo Res modular couch by Ron Arad. Julia Roberts was an idiot, I detested that stupid Cheshire grin of hers, but she sure got her way with men. At one point, when Julia and hunky Richard Gere were getting down to it, Mom nudged me. Completely out of context, she interjected, "Let's go visit Grampy tomorrow. When your homework is done."

Her timing was way strange. But I shrugged. "Sure." Fine with me.

Sunday visits with my grandfather were typically interspersed with the high noon service at Calvary Chapel. Once all my college apps were in, Mom had said I didn't have to go to church every week. She even let me quit teaching God Knows Us classes. All spring, Mom and I had been sitting in our respective pews less and less often. Fine with me.

Eventually, Mom wandered off to bed. Nobody called or rang the doorbell or anything. Saturday Night Live at the Hellers'.

I popped out the DVD and turned off our 42-inch Viera LCD HDTV. Upstairs, I closed up my laptop and lay down on my bed.

Immediately, I fell into a deep sleep. I had a ton of weird dreams that night. Maybe from the wine hangover. I'd never been much of a dreamer. Usually, I'd work at my desk until I could no longer hold my head up, then plunge into a dreamless sleep until my alarm went off at six. At least, that was the pattern before I became an insomniac. Which is what happened to me AH.

But that night, I had a dream. You'll find this interesting. It's a dream I've had more than once, but the first time was on that hungover night.

The dream's always the same, it always has a bunch of Barbie dolls in it. They all wear Lilly Pulitzer dresses and golden South Sea all-natural pearls. They kind of look like Mom. Shoulder length reddish hair, pop-out eyes, washed up cheerleader looks. In the dream, the dolls are lined up on my bed, propped against my velvet tufted wingback upholstered headboard (in wood rose). I stand there, not sure what I'm doing. H8er hurries into the room. She looks at me weird and says something like, "Grow up, Heidi." Sometimes she grabs one of the dolls. Sometimes she bites the head off and eats it.

Whatever that means.

Six: LOL

MOM SLEPT LATE. I finalized my English paper, did some reading in my deadly dull econ text, wrote an article for the *Sounder* on racial bias at Central High. It was there all right, but nobody wanted us students to talk about it because that made the school look bad and could negatively impact our funding. I spoke my mind, saved the file. Then I surfed the Internet.

HuffPo wondered: *Can Laughter Count as Exercise?*

Something to think about.

H8er IM-ed me, "Sorry @ last nite. Got hung up."

I IM-ed back, "No prob. Rain check?"

She said, "*Rain check?* LOL, fag."

I got off and went downstairs to eat lunch.

Grampy lives on a kind of ranch for oldsters out in the Everglades. He has his own one-room bungalow, but the residents dine in a centrally located cafeteria and they have lots of planned activities. Mom called ahead to make sure he wasn't scheduled to go to the movies or to a mall or something, then we got ready to go.

I put on my Lucky Brand bootcut skinny jeans with knee holes and a vintage tee-shirt from Out of the Closet, the used clothing store for teens. Mom hates that place, she thinks all the clothes have ringworms and other people's skin diseases. So whenever I shopped there, I always had to lie about my purchases and tell her the clothes were Bitsy's castoffs.

On the front of the tee-shirt, which was nuclear green and had a few strategic rips, it said, *Be Yourself. Everyone Else Is Taken.* One of my fave recycles, I hung out in that shirt at home all the time, but tended not to wear it out anywhere.

Suddenly, I felt like wearing it everywhere.

Mom wore a short-sleeved blue lace Jeanette dress with floral embroidery on mesh. By Lilly Pulitzer. No pearls, but still, it gave me a freaky rush when she strutted into the kitchen. She had on stone-embellished strappy sandals with a three-inch stacked wedge heel. Also by Pulitzer.

"You're going in *that?*" The usual start to our usual what-is-the-appropriate-dress discussion. We had our differences and neither of us held back. Today it was my turn to nag. "Grampy lives on a *ranch,* Mom. Like with horses. And llamas. And goat dung. Real live gators. Mud and muck."

She shrugged, tossed her wet hair. She was fresh from the shower and smelled like orange blossoms. "It's an old folks home with ranch *pretensions.* Besides, we're meeting Marc after we visit Grampy. For a drink."

"What does *we* mean? *I'm* not going. No way." Now I was really freaking. Was she kidding?

"He wants to meet you. I've told him what a gifted writer you are. He's *interested,* Heidi."

In my Mom's self-designed and unbreakable Book of Rules for Girls, a man's interest was the most important thing in the world. But not in my book. In my book, dignity was tops. Followed by personal freedom. And maybe truth. No, scratch that. Truth was too abstract.

In this instance, however, the truth was obvious: my

dignity would be totally trashed if I had to sit in a restaurant or somewhere else public with the two of them. It was also a matter of personal freedom. Mom's whoring was interfering with my education. If their affair lasted until fall semester, I would probably have to change my major. Just to avoid the guy my mom was banging. Thus, I did not want to go out for a drink with them. Not now. Not ever.

"*Please* don't call me Heidi in front of anyone, Mom. I've asked you not to call me that for years now. It's totally *embarrassing*."

"Who's here, Aim? Nobody but us chickens." She clucked while pouring herself a cup of coffee. She dumped in at least a hundred calories worth of Coffee-Mate Natural Bliss Lowfat Vanilla coffee creamer. Then she perched her trim rear on the black bar stool and gave me the look. The one that meant *Please, Aimee, do it for me.*

I sighed loudly before inhaling the last bite of my almond butter sandwich on flaxseed bread. Outside, someone was hitting it hard with a weed whacker. Probably Trixie, our next door neighbor. The local trannie and weekend garden warrior.

"Not going. I have tons more homework to do. I need to come straight home after we see Grampy," I lied.

"Please, hon. No fighting this morning. And calm down. Your neck is perspiring."

This was one of her sneaky little insults. It really bugged me, for some reason, and she knew it. She lowered her voice to a pseudo-soothe. "Look, Aimee. I told Marcus we'd be out west visiting relatives and he *begged* me to meet him out that way after. I promise, we won't stay long. Thirty minutes, *tops*."

Shit. I shrugged, gave in. As always. But inside, a tiny ember was burning. *SMD, Mom.*

57

"You'll love him, Aimee. And he'll love you. You two have so much in common."

She had no idea what she was saying. What a fool.

When she finished her white coffee, we left for Retiree Ranch. I waved to Trixie when we drove past. She was standing on a stepladder, trimming the ficus hedges that lined the boundary between our houses. She had on a fluorescent orange bikini top like the lifeguards wear. It looked like her hormone treatments were really kicking in.

"It's dollar shot night every night at Bill's Filling Station down in Wilton Manors," Mom said. Her way of insulting our gay neighbor. Gay, transgender, whatever.

"Lady Gaga performed there," I shot back. "Trixie has aspirations."

"I told you to stay away from him," my mother warned me. Like homosexuality was contagious.

"Her," I said. My mother the homophobe.

"*She's* troubled," my mother said as we approached the empty guard gate. "Keep your distance."

I shrugged. Trixie didn't seem the least bit troubled to me. But, whatever. My mother didn't say anything when I turned on NPR.

Grampy was sitting in a rocker on the front porch with a Remington 12-gauge shotgun in his lap. One hand on the stock, the other on the barrel. He let out a yelp as we walked up the flagstone path to his bungalow.

"Yeehaw. Got me a ugly old possum this morning," he yelled. "Right between its beady little eyes."

I kissed him on his freckled bald spot and Mom leaned in to smooch his wrinkled cheek. When she wiped off the lipstick stain with her thumb after, he grabbed her hand and gave her a quick once over.

"Where you going in that get-up? To a fashion show in the combat zone?"

Grampy liked to pick on Mom. But today she was in a good mood, the kind of mood nobody could ruin. Except, of course, the source of her joy, the new man. Her mood was always dependent on some stupid guy.

"How are *you* doing, Dad? How's your foot?"

"Foot? What about my foot?" He turned to me. I was leaning against the wooden railing that surrounded the porch. "Who's this? Your friend Agnes? She looks different."

"It's me, Grampy. Aimee."

He smiled. He wasn't wearing a bottom denture so his chin caved in. It looked dark and scary in there. "Oh, yes. *Aimee.* I didn't recognize you for a minute. You're all grown up. And so beautiful, young lady."

We smiled at one another. I wasn't sure he knew who I was, but he meant well. He said the same sort of thing almost every time we visited. And we visited him almost every week.

Mom was crouching down, examining Grampy's left leg. He was always getting these really gruesome ulcers. Because his skin was so thin. He'd go hiking around in the glades where the grasses are tall, sharp, sometimes serrated. And come home with wicked scrapes and deep cuts that didn't heal well. It was an age thing. My mom was the last of his kids and he'd been pretty old when she was born. He's ninety-two. You do the math.

"This looks a little infected, Dad," Mom said.

"Aw, it's nothin'. Leave 'er alone, dear. Come on inside, I'll get us some lemonade."

59

"I'll get it, Grampy," I offered.

Mom smiled at me and I pushed in through the screen door.

The bungalow was cool and dark. Grampy kept his Bahama shutters down and the AC blasting all year round. The house was small, a single high-ceilinged room with a cot in one corner, a saggy patchwork sofa in front of a wide-screen TV, and a kitchenette along the back wall. The bath was tiny, just a narrow shower stall and a toilet. The sink was outside the bathroom, next to Grampy's gun closet. Which was a retrofitted linen closet. He'd removed most of the shelves and filled it with his firearms collection.

I liked my grandfather's place. The floors were black slate, the walls a bright white. The house was devoid of knickknacks and doodads. No designer anything. Clean and simple. There was a stone fireplace too, with an old rifle hanging above the mantle.

Grampy's pure unadulterated Swiss. In case you don't know, the men in Switzerland all do a stint in the army after high school. At the age of eighteen, all male citizens must undergo military training. Then they're sent home with their army guns. For protection of the state. Since the Swiss never go to war, they have a lot of guns lying around. They don't go nuts over there and start shooting up strangers. They don't freak out, grab their guns, and blow people away. Not like we do here in America. Home of the free to kill.

I got the plastic pitcher of lemonade out of the little half-fridge and grabbed us three to-go cups from the cabinet above the sink. The kitchen smelled like something had gone rotten. I held my breath. What did fresh possum meat smell like? I didn't want to know the answer to that.

We sat around on Grampy's porch sipping lemonade. It needed more sugar or something. Mom made small talk and Grampy grunted every once in a while. She bandaged his leg up and he complained about it. I stared out at the cloudless blue, watching for snail kites. I liked the way they dove through the air, their v-shaped tails cutting the sky into chunks.

A group of turkey vultures circled overhead. I pointed them out to Grampy and he nodded.

"They're waiting until that ugly old possum I shot's dead enough to eat. Not sure why he's still hangin' on. I thought I gave him a decent blast."

Mom caught my eye. *He only thinks he's out there firing his guns,* she told me with her scrunched face.

"Could you give me lessons? Target lessons? You used to when I was a little kid. When you and Grammy lived in Turtle Bay. Remember?"

"Course I remember, honey. You were a good shot, too, I remember that."

"We have to get going pretty soon, Dad. Aimee has a lot of homework," Mom said.

Grampy ignored her. "Everybody in this lily-ass country should take the time to learn how to use firearms safely. Citizens everywhere need to be able to protect themselves. From home invaders, crazy people, drug dealers and gang bangers. From their own government, if need be. You want a lesson right now, kiddo? We can start with this one right here."

He held up the shotgun and waved it around. My mother and I ducked.

"That thing isn't loaded, is it, Dad?"

"You bet your busy French ass it's loaded. I'm not setting here all day like gator bait. I got to be prepared. We got black bears and Florida panthers, even them twenty-foot Burmese pythons. There's a lotta wildlife hiding out there in the brush, girls. And just last week, Fred Marple was beat almost to death by some punks at the 7-Eleven."

His small face had turned two shades of red, but he'd stopped swinging the gun. It rested in his lap like a friendly puppy.

"Fred Marple died in 1997, Dad. In Hialeah. Not up here on Retiree Ranch. You're safe as can be." Mom grinned at me. "The biggest crime you've got around here is wife swapping. That, and illegal betting on Bingo."

"Okay, suit yourself, Marlene. But your friend Agnes wants to learn how to shoot. And if she comes to visit without you, I'm gonna teach her."

He winked at me. I winked back.

Mom called Professor Dimitri from the car. She put him on speaker phone. Like that would make me feel included in their icky flirtation games. Ugh. Gag me.

"Hey, baby. We're on our way east now. Where're *you?*"

"Hello, hello. Right on time."

His voice was charred, kind of hip-DJ or ex-drug-addict sexy. I perked up and Mom caught it. She gave me a look that said *See what I mean?* I immediately slumped back in my seat and looked out the window.

Grass, nothing but tall clumps of brown grass. A few fat alligators sunning themselves on the low banks of the narrow canal weaving through the grasses. Here and there, a sprinkling of bleached white egrets or ibis, perched delicately in the skinny leafless trees. And blue sky as far as you could see. I rolled my window down to sniff the air. It smelled like gunpowder. Or burnt matches tossed on a pile of old newspapers, just starting to catch fire. I rolled it back up.

"Where do we meet you?" My mom sounded like she was building up to a big orgasm just talking to him. So gross.

"I'm waiting for you. At the Wine Deck. Where exactly are you, babe?"

I hate it when men call women *babe*. The only thing worse is when they call women *sugar*.

"Oh, I *love* the Deck," She purred. "*Perfect*." She was flattering him. The Wine Deck is a dump. "We're not far. On 60, heading your way at the upper level of legal. So maybe we're ten minutes out?"

He grunted. Then nothing. So brilliant. A stimulating conversationalist. I couldn't imagine sitting with the two of them for more than five minutes. A car accident would be preferable. Inside my head, I yelled, *Come on, somebody mow us down!*

"What're you drinking, Marc? I want to imagine your lips on the glass. I want to imagine the taste."

I cringed. Did she have to say stuff like that in public?

"A superb 1998 Chateauneuf-du-Pape. Ever try it, sugar?"

I threw up a little in my mouth. It tasted like almond butter and lemons. And way leftover rioja. If I had to sit there and watch them say stupid stuff and drink a bunch of overpriced snob wine, I would totally blow cookies.

Mom said, "Sounds yummy. Can you order a Coke Zero with crushed ice for Aimee? We'll see you soon."

She made kissing noises. To his credit, he laughed.

Seven: Meeting John Varvatos
(A One Act Play)

PURELY FOR ENTERTAINMENT purposes, I am presenting to you a summary of my first meeting with Mom's newest man and my future writing professor. For reasons of individual creativity, this summary comes in the form of a short play. Believe me, I understand that my life has become a tragedy of epic proportions. But some parts are kind of funny. You like my sense of humor. You told me that once. See, I remember stuff like that.

Setting: The Wine Deck, mid-afternoon, a warm Sunday in April
Characters: Me, Mom, Professor Dimitri; Bradley, a cute twenty-something waiter; H8er.
Details: Other people are eating lunch at the picnic tables around us, but they're all extras; they make background noise, along with several swooping osprey calling out for mates or fish or something, and the overwhelming roar of approaching and departing airboats. Think: Everglades chic.

Mom: You're absolutely right, Marc. This is the best Bordeaux I've ever had! So robust.
Marc: Glad you like it.

Me: And my Coke Zero is like Beaujolais. So fresh! And *lively*. The flavor lingers in the mouth like *bile*.

[I don't say this out loud, of course. In fact, I don't say much at all to Professor Dimitri. I'm way too intimidated. Plus, I can be good at saying nothing when I want to, too. Just like H8er.]

Marc: How's your father, Marlene?

Mom: Good. He's amazing for his age. Still so *physical*. He hikes around with his World War II rifles, his back country shotguns, tracking wild *animals*. Out in the *Glades*. If you can believe that.

Marc: Sounds like a character out of a Harry Crews novel.

Me: Harry Crews? Now there's a man's man. Guns, drinking binges, virile insanity, rages which often include the beating of women about the face. Is this the kind of craptastic literature I'll be reading in your classes, Professor D?

[No, no, of course I don't say these words out loud. But here I must add a note about Professor Dimitri. He's dressed head to foot in John Varvatos. Flight pants in a pale khaki, linen shirt with pleated front in a soft gray. Retro sunglasses, tortoise shell with little guitar heads on the frames. A black leather lariat with silver tips. High-top Converse sneakers in navy blue. He's hilarious. Who does he think he is, Green Day? He has nice hair, though, streaked blond and down over his collar, thick. He's tan, handsome in a goofy, older guy way. His body is okay, too, sort of jogged trim, a tiny bit buffed. It's just too damn bad he's a walking cliché for mid-life crisis. He even drives a red convertible. Miata. Cheapest sports car on the market. Mom pointed it out in the parking lot like it was next year's model Ferrari. Poor Mom. No taste. Still, Professor Dimitri scares me. Department head, writing teacher, authority over my future. And he's seeing my mother? I'm tongue tied and the adrenaline is fast-pumping around in my bloodstream.]

Mom: Aimee, tell Marc about the paper you're working on. An English poet, right? (to Marcus) For one of her classes at HSC this semester. Intro to Literature. I think I told you about that the other night, right? I was a little . . . um, hee hee . . . *tipsy*.

Marcus: Who do you have, Aimee? Professor Whitehead?

Bradley: Hi ladies, I'm Bradley. I'll be your waiter today. I see you already have your drinks. Will either of you be dining today?

Mom: Nothing for me. This wine is *superb*, though.

Marcus: Aimee? Would you like a burger or something? They have a kids' menu.

Me: Do you serve Happy Meals here? With plastic toys?

[Of course, I don't say that. I can barely speak, my mortification so thick in my throat. I shake my head at the cute waiter. His teeth are too even. Excessive orthodontics, possibly. My cheeks are warm. Mom notices and pretends not to. Marcus shrugs, smiles helplessly at Bradley. *Kids these days, you can't please them.* Bradley leaves after giving Marcus a sly grin. Former student? Or did they talk before we got here? Whatever, something passes between them. I'm starting to dislike Professor Dimitri. He's a type. The type of prof that wants the coolest kids to worship him, but doesn't give a shit about the rest of us. The ember in my gut flares, reminds me of its fiery existence.]

Mom: Aimee writes for the *Hope Shore Sounder*. Guest articles. They have a weekly column for student opinion. Are you familiar with it, Marc?

Marc: Oh, sure. Some of my students write for the *Sounder*. I've been known to send the paper a piece of my mind now and again myself. Letters to the editor, you know.

Mom: Ooooh, that's interesting! What topics have you written on? Maybe we've read your work!

Me: Big fucking deal. You write freelance for the *Sounder*? Scoff. What about your giant erection of a make-me-famous book deal, Professor D? How's that coming along?

[Not that I say this. I'm silent. Mom's all excited. Her eyes poke out. I can see them bugging behind her shades. She's practically panting. She has one hand on her wine glass, the other one under the table. Probably on his leg. Ick. I suck uselessly on my straw, look around the deck. Everyone else is eating huge arugula salads or giant blood-dripping burgers. I'm hungry but I'm not staying here a minute longer than I have to. Food orders would take way too long. This little visit is going to be just like Mom promised. It's going to last thirty minutes, *tops*. I turn on my iPhone to check the time. There's a text message waiting.]

H8er: WTF r u doin up there?

[I look around quickly. Parents with toddlers, couples in tanks and baggies, an elderly pair of women drinking green tea, a group of church types with bonnets and long Laura-Ashley-style dresses. Then I peer over the wooden railing and scan down the boat dock until I spot a familiar shock of white hair. H8er.]

Me: (to Mom) 'Scuse me, I see someone I know. Can I be excused?

Mom: Sure, honey. Who is it? Anybody I know?

Me: New friend of mine. Back in a minute.

Mom: She has a *ton* of friends. From track, church, school. I can't *possibly* keep up.

Marcus: Um hmm.

Mom: So tell me about your day yesterday, Marc. What did you do after we . . . hee hee . . . after I left? Did you think about me?

[Gagging slightly, I rush across the restaurant deck and down the rickety wooden stairs to the dock. Two airboats rock on the murky, grassy river. In the distance, you can hear one coming. Airboat rides into the Everglades are popular with tourists. Especially the older, hard of hearing folks who don't mind the ear-shattering scream of a high horsepower aircraft engine.

H8er has moved from the spot right below my mom's table to a slatted bench at the end of the dock. I sit down beside her and we knock fists. Her fingers are freshly tattooed with tiny letters that are hard to read. She's wearing my h.i.p. hot pink crochet-back slouchy top from Nordstrom's. So last-year's-style that I didn't even miss it when I checked what she'd taken from my closet. She's still got on her disgusting ripped-to-shit shorts. Her hair is clean, her feet filthy. She looks good from the waist up.]

Me: Is it my imagination or are you following me?

H8er: I'm conducting an ethnography, so I'm trying to blend into your life. Study the inner workings of nerd world.

Me: Seriously. What are you doing here?

H8er: Same thing you are. Dying of fucking boredom.

Me: You got inked up.

H8er: You ain't seen nuthin' yet. (Yanks front of pants down to show off Chinese symbol low on belly.)

Me: (Wincing) Nice ink. What's it mean?

H8er: It means I'm a stupid twat. Whaddya think it means, Heller?

Me: Um. (Looking around) Are you here by yourself?

H8er: Give me a break. (Pause) Who's the dick up on deck?

Me: My mom's boyfriend.

H8er: The one she fucked Friday night?

Me: That would be the one.

H8er: I could go for some of that.

Me: Gross out. He's like fifty trying to play twenty-five.

H8er: He's not so bad. Your mom could do worse. She's a bit of a fox herself.

Me: Right. Fox. Mom. I feel pukey.

H8er: Get the double burger with Gruyère cheese. That'll make the nausea go away.

Me: If I eat anything, they'll keep talking. I don't think I can stand it much longer.

H8er: Didn't you say he's a writer? What has he written? Anything hot?

Me: No. He's a loser. But I'll have to take his class in the fall. If I'm at HSC.

H8er: You will be. But that's okay. You not going to some fancy pants college is a nice kick in the balls for your mom. That should feel pretty good.

Me: Why would it? She's on my side. She wants the best for me, for my future. She wants me to go to the best school so I can land a good job.

H8er: Unlike her, Miss Realtor of the Month for Nowhere Developments, U.S.A.? No, she wants you to attend Brown or some other snob school just so she can brag about you to her fuck buddies. So they'll think better of her. Like you're not just an extension of her own inadequacy.

Me: Wow. You really think you have us all figured out. I didn't know you majored in psychobabble.

H8er: Here's what the therapist recommends. Go back up there and flirt with her boyfriend. Sit with your legs open. Lick your fingers. See if he hits on you. That'll liven things up.

Me: Oh please. He just asked me if I wanted the kids' menu. I can't flirt with him.

H8er: He did that to make your mom think he sees you as a child. So she won't feel threatened. You look hot today. Go give him a little Lolita thrill.

Me: Ick. But I gotta go back. Come with. Meet my mom.

H8er: Not today. I'm totally stoned. I don't think I'd make the right kind of impression.

Me: She won't notice. She's all eyes for Doc Varvatos.

H8er: Think about it, Heller. Are you sure you want me to meet her with these on? (Holds up a bare foot caked with grime.) And these? (Waves her finger tats which, I now see upon careful examination, spell out "suck my dick" in navy block print letters, one per finger.)

Me: Good point.

H8er: Go on. Text ya lata'. I have a fucking ballzy idea. For next weekend.

Me: 'kay.

H8er: And don't be a total fem. Strap on a pair for once. Go play Candyland, give the old guy a little something to dream on.

Me: Yeah, right.

[I leave her sitting there on the bench and I drag myself along real slow, making my way gradually back down the dock and up the wooden stairs. What feels like an intolerably long while later, H8er saunters past our table. I'm zoning out and

Mom is yakking and Professor D is drinking his wine in some kind of new boyfriend stupor. They are driving me UTFW— up the friggin' wall. Seeing H8er cheers me. I wave but H8er keeps going. She totally ignores me.]

Mom: (Flipping her head around like an owl.) Who are you waving to?

Me: Friend of mine. I'll introduce you some other time. When we're not on a date.

Marcus: Shall we? (The bottle is empty, he's pointing this out.)

Mom: I'm driving. I can't. And Aimee has to get home. She has homework.

Marcus: (Signaling) Bradley? Can we have the check, dude?

Me: Thank god. Get me the fuck out of here. Prof Dude is such a poser.

[Of course, I don't say this to anyone. I just smile blandly, stand up. If we leave right now, I can see where H8er went. Once she disappeared into the dusty parking lot, I lost track of her.]

Me: I'll drive, Mom. (I hold out my hand and she gives me the keys.)

Me again: Nice meeting you, Professor Dimitri. See you on campus.

Marcus: We should sit down next month, after finals are over. Talk about what you want to achieve at college. Maybe I can point out some ways to enhance your experience at HSC. I can give you a few tips on what to look for, who to avoid. (He's smiling, faking interest in me.)

Mom: Isn't that *sweet*. You'd do that for *us*? (She leans into him, says to me:) Be there in a minute, Heidi.

[*Heidi? Fuck me, Mom*. I hurry out to the lot and look for

H8er. She's nowhere. When I turn back, the two lovebirds are standing beside our table. They're hugging and my prof has his hands all over my mother's nice tight jogger's ass. He's running his tanned, manicured hand up and down, rubbing around, squeezing her butt like a peach. Disgusting. I use the remote to click open the car door and duck inside. I check the time on the dashboard and it's been a full hour and a half since we pulled into this lot. Evidence for the upcoming prosecution. I'll use this against my mother all the way home. Leverage.]

Mom: Well? (We're en route. She's got her head back against the head rest.)

Me: Well what? (Making her suffer.)

Mom: You know. *Marc.* So? Tell. What do you *think?*

Me: He's okay. Can I like get my license next week? Pleeeeze, Moms? See how safe I'm driving?

Mom: Oh, Aim. I don't know. I'm just not ready to ask Uncle Moneybags for a new car for you. How-bout after you graduate?

Me: We can like share the Land Rover, I don't care. I just think it would be good for both of us if I had my driver's license. We can take turns, like I can drop you off at work one day and then, the next day, you can drop me at HSC? Or Central, wherever I have to go? So you don't have to drive me everywhere all the time, right? I mean, it would be like so much easier on you. Especially this summer when I'll have to be at HSC every day.

Mom: I don't know, honey. It's a *big* step and I don't like how the kids drive at *either* school and, well, I trust *you* but, you know.

Me: That was an hour and a half, you know. Your "have a drink with Marc". Your "half hour, tops". Right? A whole *hour*

72

and a half out of my day. And I have a ton of homework to do before tomorrow. I'll be up half the night now cuz of that.

Mom: I know, baby. You were *so* good about it. Thank you, *thank you!* (Air kisses) He's gonna be a *huge* help to you with your writing, you watch. And don't you think he's *gorgeous?* (Heavy sighs)

Me: He's a hottie, Moms. So can we like make an appointment at the DMV? How's next Friday? No track! It's Good Friday, Passover and Easter weekend! I'm totally free! Timing is perfect, right?

Mom: Oh, Aim. I don't know. Maybe? Can't we decide later? My head is spinning. (Pause) Doesn't he have a wonderful *voice?* So deep, so damn *sexy.* (More sighs)

[This kind of thing continues for the twenty minute drive home. When we reach the front gate at Palm Ridge Hills, both of us have had it with putting the other off and trying to be nice about it. I'm pretty good at it, Mom's like a professional.]

Me: How'd I do? Perfect, right? My driving is like perfect.

Mom: Umm. So how does Chinese sound? I really don't feel like cooking tonight.

Me: If I had my license, I could go to Paisley's and pick up something. We could eat good stuff every night and you could just relax.

Mom: Can we place a temporary moratorium on this subject? My head's going to explode, Aim. I mean it.

[When I check my iPhone later, there's a message from H8er. I call her back. She's whispering so it's hard to hear what she's saying.]

H8er: Tell your mom I hitched a ride home with her boyfriend. He's a keeper!

Me: Bullshit. Where are you?

H8er: Stopped off to have a little road sex. (Pant, pant) The Miata's just not big enough for the both of us. (Laughs softly.)

Me: You lie.

H8er: On my back. Whenever I can. (Laughs loudly, hangs up.)

Eight: Boy Finds Live Grenade
On Easter Egg Hunt

T HAT WAS THE HuffPo headline on Sunday. Caught my eye.

I was waiting for Mom to get ready for church. I couldn't believe I was headed to Calvary Chapel with Mom. Not after the weekend I'd just spent with H8er. My soul report card had gone from excellent lily white to black as sin and piss poor. In only thirty-six hours. WWGD about the likes of me?

What Would God Do? Nothing. Continue to ignore me. Like He had for the past seventeen years.

H8er texted me: "Heard the good newz?"

I texted back: "He is rizen." Then I turned off my iPhone and my laptop and ran down the stairs to the garage. Mom was sitting in the passenger seat. As soon as I passed the test on Friday and got my warm, freshly sealed in plastic driver's license, she folded. She'd just smiled at me, kind of sadly, nostalgic maybe, and handed over the keys. Since then she'd spent our drive time texting and checking her phone for messages. From guess who.

The Land Rover roared gracefully to life and I backed out of the driveway after looking carefully in both directions. If Mom had seen the way I drove on Friday night, she wouldn't have sat there texting with a lovesick smile on her face. She'd be behind the wheel and I'd be at home on lockdown.

Before my college rejection/wait list letters began arriving in the mail, I'd spent a lot of my time on lockdown: no phone, no Facebook, no TV, no shopping, no nothing but studying. Nose to the screen, unless I was busy scoring points with extracurriculars. Sports team, editorial team, volunteering team. Or nose to the screen. This was my life for three and a half years of high school. Mom's secret method to transform a nerdy but no genius kid like me into Ivy League material. A plan that proved to be massive fail.

Upside was, I'd been off lockdown for weeks now. With H8er in my life, however, I knew I could be headed right back to the isolation ward. If I valued my freedom, which I thought sure I did, I'd have to be much, much more careful.

I pulled down the visor and tried to keep the morning sun out of my eyes. My brain was pounding against my skull like it wanted out. Another weekend-long hangover. H8er was nothing if not a consistently bad influence. Of course, she could cast the blame on *me* for our antics together, but she didn't. Why bother? We both knew she was basically my private tutor on badness, urging me to break out of what she called *Nerdvana*. After all, I'd been stuck for years in the super-grind's nirvana for nerds. And really, how could I argue with her about that? I wasn't good at defending my life. It had long felt like somebody else's version of my life anyway. Even I knew myself well enough to know that I needed some serious breaking out.

Dangerous, but necessary. That's what I told myself at the time. Dangerous, but necessary.

After we passed the guard gate, Mom said without looking up from her texting, both thumbs flying, "I found something this morning when I got back from Boca. I believe you owe me an explanation, Aimee."

My roiling gut slammed south and I felt like shit. Literally. I didn't know what Mom had found but I sure could imagine. The empty bottle of 1993 J Schram champagne? An itty bitty roach? A crumpled pack of Newports? A package of ribbed condoms?

I gritted my teeth, the wheel, and my anal sphincter, and kept my eyes on the road, driving steadily down Ocean Boulevard. There was a lot of traffic. All us heathens were out at once, making our annual Easter pilgrimage. What a bunch of hypocrites.

Mom slipped her smart phone into the slash pocket of her red polished leather Capri Satchel with gold chain straps. Gucci. She leaned forward and snapped off the radio, even though it was obvious I'd been listening to NPR.

"Now is not the time to discuss it. Not on the way to church. But Aimee, I just cannot understand why you would listen to such garbage."

She shook her head, despairing at my horrible taste. The maroon and gold baubles on her Mark Davis Luna Hair Clip bounced gaily. I watched her out of the corner of my eye. How mad was she?

"Listen to what? This segment? I like NPR, Moms," I said.

One of our many diffs. Mom preferred FOX. Less gab, more gore, she liked to say when she sat down to watch the evening news.

"Not the radio, Aimee. Your taste in music."

My taste in music? Relief flooded through me, unwinding the tension from my hands to my intestines. I relaxed my grip on the hand-stitched leather steering wheel cover. My palms stopped sweating.

77

"Marilyn Manson is a known *satanist*, Aimee. What, have you suddenly developed *goth* leanings? From all that *poetry* you've been reading? Is *that* what's going on?"

Inside my hammering skull, part of me was laughing, but I managed to say *très* calmly, "Oh *that*. A friend loaned me that CD. Awful, isn't it?"

"I wouldn't know. I absolutely refuse to even listen to that, that . . . *weirdo*. But which friend of yours has such dark sensibilities? Not Bitsy?"

Wouldn't that freak Mom out, if I told her Bitsy had become a satanist? I considered it for a second, but then I couldn't help it. I snickered. I'm such a terrible liar, I could never pull off a whopper like that.

"Oh, I guess *that's* unlikely," my mom said with a little laugh. "So whose is it? Now I'm curious."

But when a text suddenly arrived, she returned to her online conversation. With Dr. Dude, I assumed. They'd been together all weekend, and yet, she kept up the communication. Because my mother needed the constant reassurance that he was still interested in her. That she was *interesting* enough to keep him engaged in one long, pointless, apparently endless conversation.

Such a massive waste of personal energy.

I took a right on Church Street. At least I was off the hook. I'd have to remember to keep the CDs in my room after all future lost weekends. H8er loved Marilyn Manson. And Metallica. Ozzy Osbourne. Old Sex Pistols. All the really bleak, suicidal, wracked with mayhem and hate music. Which suited her.

Me, I could take it or leave it. All that darkness. I kind of preferred soft rock. Doofus me. But I indulged my new

friend. Tried to remain open to her ideas and influences.
   Me, breaking out.

What had gone down was this. We'd IM-ed and texted all
week, making the wildest plans imaginable for Easter weekend.
On Friday night, after I dropped Mom at the Hyatt Spa and
Pool Bar, where she was meeting Professor Dimitri for a drink
that would evolve into a weekend at his condo, I picked up
H8er at the bus station downtown.
   "Yo," she said when she climbed into the passenger seat.
Her voice sounded slurry. "S'up?"
   "WTF, H8er?" I tried not to stare. I needed to keep my
eyes on the happy hour drivers around us.
   She looked bad. Worse than ever. Her top lip was swollen
with a recently added silver ball stud. She stuck out her tongue
so I could see the matching stud there. Ugh. She was like a
walking bacterial infection. My nice slouchy shirt had what
looked like grass stains down the front and was as filthy as
her shorts and feet. She smelled like reefer and grilled onions.
   "First we go to my house and you get cleaned up," I said.
"PU."
   "Uh, FU, Heller? But I got no problem wid dat. I like
your nice big shower with all the swiveling shower heads. I
can practically come if I aim them just right." She laughed.
"And your fucking walk-in with shelf after shelf of fucking
ultra-luxe snob clothes? To die for." She glanced at me.
"You'll need to fix yourself too, Heller. Unless you're
changing the plans and we're going to a fucking Girl Scout
convention."
   I laughed. "No worries there. While you're cleaning up, I'm
gonna invade my mom's walk-in. Believe me, that and a dip in

her jewelry box, plus ten minutes at her makeup mirror, and I'll look like a major slut."

"Right on, Aimee. You go, girlfriend," H8er mocked.

"Are you pissed I said you smell bad?"

"No. I'm just hungry. And thirsty. Pissy."

"And bored," we said at the same time, then laughed together.

"It's fucking Friday night, Heller," H8er chanted as we cruised down A1A in my mom's luxury SUV.

My heartbeat sped up. I was kind of excited. We'd made a lot of crazy plans, and maybe most of them were just girls talking. But I knew something was sure to happen that weekend. I had my freedom while Mom was distracted by Professor Dimitri's "big suckable cock" (according to H8er, who was, I thought, like majorly lying about even meeting him). So surely something fun was going to happen. Something I could remember for the rest of my life. Something unlike what Aimee Heller, goodie-goodie nerd girl, had ever experienced before.

"Par*tay*," I said.

What I really meant was, I *am free of Mom*.

Mom sat in the back row pew at Calvary, which was less packed than I'd expected. Maybe because we were twenty minutes early. Another surprise was she didn't make me sit up front with the born-agains, and for that I could have kissed her.

As usual, she read USA *Today* on her phone and I sat there on the hard wooden seat designed to make you think about your rotten inner life. Just being there in church, trapped on a stiff bench in a sunlit room, stuck inside my own head for like an hour with a lot of godly talk and godly songs in the air around me, had always made me feel repentant. Even when I had nothing to repent.

But not anymore. Now I had lots to apologize to God for. And how did I feel?

I felt *awesome*. Except for the hangover, the creeping advance of another slammer migraine, and a tender rawness between my legs, I felt fucking awesome.

We'd dressed H8er last. She borrowed a pair of my mom's leggings. (Her legs are way longer than mine so my pants don't fit her right.) Forest green velvet AG Adriano Goldschmied stretch pants from Bloomingdale's. They looked great paired with my cream-colored Cowl-Neck Cashmere Sweater from Neiman Marcus and a matching pair of UGG's Australia Classic Tall pull-on boots with sheepskin lining. She didn't want to carry a purse, though.

"Too fem," she said. "Besides, you'll be carrying the money. And I'll keep the smokes in my waistband. Which looks thuggie, right?"

"Oh yeah. Right." Thuggie? Whatever. "But what about your ID? How will we get in anywhere without at least one fake ID?" I mean, I sure didn't have one.

H8er was glugging from one of my mom's Vera Wang Duchesse champagne flutes. We'd popped open a bottle after our showers. I didn't know anything about champagne, so it could have been worth hundreds of dollars or only twenty-five. The bottle had been sitting in a gold velour gift box on a low shelf in the fridge for like years. I was hoping Mom wouldn't reach back there anytime soon and notice what was now an empty box. If she did, she would be ripshit.

The bubbly went down fast and the sweetness made me giddy. I really didn't care if we got into a bar or not. Dressing up while drinking champagne out of crystal flutes was my kind of fun.

H8er was caking on the green eyeliner. She looked like a Persian cat. In a painting by Picasso.

"I told you, that waiter at the Wine Deck will serve us. He gave me the old dick-eye last weekend. I'll give him a knob job if I have to. You watch."

"No, thanks," I said, handing her my mom's Antik Batik Kivas Feather and Chain necklace, a gift from Uncle Moneybags after Mom sold her first house. I think Dads was hopeful she'd be supporting us herself after that. But she couldn't. I mean, she made okay money, but not enough to pay for our lifestyle.

"And you'll need to carry the condoms, Heller. We can stop at CVS on the way to the Deck."

I almost poked my eye out with a mascara brush. Ick. Even the idea of touching a condom grossed me out. Never mind what would be in one. Ew.

"*I'm* not buying condoms, H8er. No way, Jose. *You'll* have to go in and get them. I'll give you the money. Besides, I wouldn't know what kind to choose. You're the sexpert."

A little chill ran down my arms, made me goose pimple up. I was grossed out, but excited.

H8er snorted. "SMD, pussy. Let's get rolling. I'm hungry, thirsty, pissy and . . ."

Long story short, H8er bought us a package of Her Pleasure Ecstasy Lubricated Trojans at the CVS on West Palmetto. She jogged out of the brightly lit store waving the blue box above her head like a flag of victory. I sank down in the driver's seat, covering my eyes with my palms. Thank god nobody else was in the strip mall parking lot.

At a nearly empty Wine Deck, our luck seemed to run out. Looking as surfer dude hot as he had the week before, Bradley was our waiter that evening. I jumped in right away and ordered a Hukilau Rum Punch. Off the top of my head, the silly Polynesian restaurant drink was all I could think of to ask for. Bradley grinned. His eyes were the same greenish blue as his polo shirt. A kind of Caribbean blue. I smiled back in what I thought was a mature manner.

Unfortunately, Bradley couldn't—or maybe wouldn't—serve us a drink. "Too conspicuous, I could get shitcanned," he said. But he did suggest trying the Sea Oat in Royal Palms. "Notorious for serving underage drinkers," he explained. Then, looking only at me, he said, "Hand me your cell."

H8er nodded at me, like *Do it, pussy.* So I handed it to him and he punched in his digits. "Call me if you get into the Oat. I'll come by after work, buy you a drink," he promised.

I flashed my best mature slut smile. H8er, grinning, led the way back to the car.

Bradley liked me? WTF? My heart fluttered happily but my brain was no-no-no-ing away. Typical. The body lusts, the mind rebels. Bradley? He was way too good-looking to make the moves on someone like me. I could have felt something like hopeful anticipation, but I didn't. I didn't feel a sense of approaching dread, either, though. I guess the champagne had made me brave.

"Nice work, Heller," H8er said after we climbed into the Land Rover. "If he isn't a total fag, he could be a nice first fuck for you."

She lit up a fat doobie and held it to my lips while I drove east toward the beach.

"Hopefully, he doesn't go to HSC," I said between coughs. "I mean, he won't show up tonight, and if he does, he won't want to do it with me. But if by some egregious fluke I do have sex with Bradley, I don't want to have to see him around campus after."

"There you go, Heller. Spoken like a major wuss."

The Sea Oat fit our needs perfectly. The bar was roomy, underlit, and trash-strewn. Patrons were mostly middle-aged men and women in black leather with paisley head scarves and life-size tattoos. I should have been scared, worried about my safety, but I felt like I was going to have a laughing fit. What a den of iniquity!

I let H8er belly up to the bar while I scuttled toward a dark corner. Sat myself down in a booth and stared down at the carved up wood table covered with pools of stale beer. I tried not to catch anyone's eye.

The bartender had a nasty sleaze, tennis ball biceps, and a close-shaved skull. He served H8er whatever she ordered for us without raising an eyebrow.

Nobody looked at us twice. We were tucked away in that orange Naugahyde booth way in the back. The seats were torn and it smelled musty.

H8er sneered at me, then shot her tequila. Lime, salt. She said, "This is da place, Heller. The management doesn't give a fifth of a fuck, they'd fill drink orders for toddlers carrying tiny fistfuls of dollar bills."

We laughed, but mostly because we were high. And drunk.

I worked my way through two Sam Adams drafts while she belted down a second and a third shot, then I sent the text.

Bradley responded almost immediately, said he'd be there in half an hour. Okay. Whatever.

My blasé attitude surprised me. If he showed up, well then, I would fuck him. If not, who cared, really? Not me.

I licked a frothing of amber beer foam from my mug while H8er danced by herself in front of the CD jukebox. Every song had the same theme: Life is sad, love doesn't last, drinking is the way to absolve your woes. Or at least to wallow in them poetically.

Somehow I lost track of the time. And place. And H8er.

When I stumbled out to the parking lot, I was way too buzzed to drive home and I wasn't sure what I was going to do about it. H8er was already outside. She waved to me coyly from the back of a midnight blue motorcycle, a big one. She had her arms around some fat guy. I stared. *What?*

They zoomed out onto the beach road, H8er hugging this burly guy with an Uncle Sam beard and black leather kickboots. WTF?

When Bradley finally pulled up in a battered silver Hyundai, I was stretched out, half-asleep, in the back seat of the Land Rover. He knocked on my window and held up a six-pack of Heineken. Just what I needed, more intoxicants.

It's sort of a blur after that, but I do remember he drank at least one bottle of beer and smoked at least one skinny joint. I took a few hits. It was some kind of super-weed, harsh and medicinal. He chain-smoked cigarettes and the smell got in my mouth and hair. When he kissed me, he stuck his tongue down my throat until I almost gagged. I remember he said something like, "You kiss like a virgin," and I laughed like a lunatic. He had to kiss me again to make me calm down.

85

I guess Bradley isn't gay. And I guess I actually fucked him. My B.

On Saturday afternoon around 4:00, I woke up alone in my bed. My head was pounding in what was becoming an all too familiar rhythm. *Beatbeatbeat, ouch ouch ouch.* I was still in my clothes. The crotch of my underpants had a bunch of dried blood, and some of it had stained my sheets. I was still bleeding a little. Ick.

Reconstructing the night before was not happening. How had I driven myself home? I could imagine the Land Rover weaving wildly down Ocean Boulevard, but the image was cartoonish, vague as a dream. Maybe Bradley had driven me home. It was all a big blank.

Groaning out loud, I dragged myself out of bed. I had to clean up: myself, my bed linens, the car, the house. H8er and I had been messy, sloppy, careless.

This kept me busy until dark.

I had just collapsed on the couch with a cup of soothing chamomile tea when the sound-barrier was pierced by the scream of a large engine motorcycle. It burst up the street, then cut out on what sounded like my front lawn.

When I opened the door, H8er stood on the landing, her back to me. Then she turned around and I freaked. Her left eye was swollen shut, eggplant purple, and her nose was bleeding. My nice sweater had stains down the front of it, blood stains. The knees of my mom's leggings were ripped. Both of them. Like she'd crawled over a barb wire fence. I could see torn flesh through the holes.

But H8er was grinning.

"Dude, tomorrow is already the tenth," she said.

"What the hell . . ."

"SMD, if it isn't my BFF, the recently deflowered *ex*-virgin," she laughed.

"How'd you know?"

She shoved by me on her way to the kitchen. For ice for her eye, wet paper towel to clean up her nose, a beer to calm her nerves.

"Written all over your face, Heller," she said, swinging open the freezer door. "Like an *I finally got laid* tat. On your forehead. In blue neon."

The notes of the last song of the Easter service still hung in the air as we slipped out of our pew and fled hundreds of churchgoers, all the good folks perched on the edge of their seats, waiting for the final blessing. In less than a minute, they would surge from the building, rushing head first from their somber piety into the generous lap of a beautiful spring day.

Mom said, "Hurry, or we'll get trapped in the lot. I saw at least *five* of my *worst* clients in there. I don't want to get stuck talking about *mortgage* rates. Not today."

We ran to the car, Mom lagging behind in her Stuart Weitzman platform pumps made in Spain. In Hummous (chickpea tan), with a three-inch heel. I still had the key so I started up the engine and shifted into drive. She jumped in and *whoosh*, we were out of there.

The sun hurt like hell. My migraine had settled in tenaciously, hanging on for a debilitating hours-long head-squeeze. I needed to lie on my back in a darkened room with a damp cloth draped across my face.

On the drive home, Mom was uncharacteristically silent. But that didn't last. It never does with her.

"Marc thinks you have talent, Aimee. He wants to look at

more of your work. Maybe for the campus literary magazine."

The traffic lights were piercing my eyeballs like heated needles. The sunlight razored my skin. I should have let Mom drive. I was still in bad shape from Friday, despite laying low on Saturday night. H8er and I had stayed home and watched her favorite movie, *The Big Lebowski*.

She claimed she'd been given the DVD by Vedder, the Harley guy, as like an apology. After he'd chased her around the dumpy ranch house he lived in with a bunch of rednecks, and somehow roughed her up. I didn't ask for details. I didn't want to know. She seemed comfortable with it. Like shit like domestic abuse happened to her all the time.

"This movie is great! Walter is such a hot head, he's such an angry asshole. You'll love him," she promised.

When I woke up, the TV was off and she was gone.

"What do you mean, more of my work, Mom? What exactly has he seen of mine?"

She had no right to show anyone my writing. Bursts of acid lurched upward from my stomach toward my epiglottis. This morning's almond butter tasted especially bad the second time around. My skull stretched tighter and tighter around its drumming contents.

"Aim, I want you to think about what I'm saying *very* carefully. Marcus could be a *godsend* for you at that little half-wit school. Yesterday he mentioned a teaching assistant position. *Paid.* He's talked about internships at local publications, grad school slots. He knows grad program directors, New York City editors. He could be *instrumental* in helping you. He can help you launch your *career.*"

I didn't know what to say. I was so confused. Was she only

sleeping with the man to help *me*? With my education, my so-called career? Totally sick. I was only seventeen, I had no real career plan. I didn't even know what I wanted out of life. I wasn't sure I ever would. Maybe I was doomed to continue to just be Marlene Heller's creation. All my life I'd been letting her create her own version of my life for me. What else did I know?

She hadn't been doing so great at the creating bit lately, though. Lit major at Hope Shore College? Big whup. But now that I'd BFF-ed H8er, I was beginning to find my own way. And maybe it was time for me to take over everything else about my life. Maybe I could feel my way along without *her* giving all the directions.

I pulled into our driveway and shut off the car. The engine clicked loudly as it cooled. Mom turned to look at me. She cocked her head, her inchworm brows peeking above the dark lens of her shades. She was expecting me to say something along the lines of *You're right, Mom; whatever you say, Mom.* Like I always did.

Instead, I said, "I'm not going to fuck him, Mom. And if this is all about me, you shouldn't keep fucking him, either."

Her jaw dropped and then her mouth snapped shut, forming a bitter line. Before I could move she reached over and slapped my face. Her oversize sterling silver and scrimshaw crew ring banged against my cheek. Tears sprang to my eyes.

This was a first. She'd never hit me before. Ever.

I opened my door and slid out. The noontime sun impaled me. I covered my bruised cheek with one hand, cradling my wound. It was all I could do to drag myself into the house without screaming insanely or spontaneously combusting.

Sometimes I really hated her.

She didn't come into my bedroom that afternoon to talk to me and change my washcloths. In fact, I didn't see her until Monday morning on the drive to school. Even then, it was awkward between us.

I took that as a sign of progress.

Nine: Crapesthetic

YOU PROBABLY THINK I'm totally lame for not being more upset about losing the V. But giving it up to a guy like Bradley, an older guy who didn't even like me, just didn't seem like such a big thing. I don't remember much about the sex itself, like I told you already, and it's not like I'm in love with the guy. I mean, he's hot, but not someone I could care about. I think he's too in love with himself. Good looking guys are like that. Professor Dimitri is another one who loves his own nicely toned ass way too much for anyone else to take seriously. My mom found that out the hard way.

And you need to understand about H8er, too. I mean, she was totally nonchalant about her face beating from Vedder. She said he'd just hauled off and smacked her for no reason. "Fucking and punching," she called it, but she smirked when she told me that. I'm guessing she did something that got him ripshit. Not that there's any worthy excuse, the guy outweighed her by like a hundred pounds. But still, H8er is the type that can really get under your skin when she wants to.

Like how she texted me like a dozen times while I was in my English Lit class at HSC the Thursday after Easter. Which bugged the crap out of me. I had to turn off my phone, which I don't like to do, because I could hear it vibrating and vibrating in my purse. Nonstop buzzing. I mean, cool it, right? When I checked my messages after class while I waited for the bus to the library, there were so many it annoyed me.

Later, on the bus with nothing to do but wait to get where I didn't want to go, I took a look at H8er's texts. And when I read them, I had to laugh. Here's what she sent me:

Brad had my virginity
And bids me to the Oat, for he
(All find safety in the tomb.)
Wanders out into the night . . .
Men come, men go:
All things remain in God.
Though like a Beach Rd.
That men pass over
My body makes no moan
But sings on:
All things remain in God.
He is rizen!

That girl could misquote with the best of the lit majors.

She called me later that afternoon while I was shelving sticky YA books. Some of them had food crumbs glued to the pages. And who knew what else. It was disgusting.

When my phone rang, I slipped behind the 92 shelving and took the call, even though socializing was against the rules for student volunteers. At this point, I wanted a reason to permanently leave my post. Mom was forcing me to continue volunteering until summer school started, but I was sick of being nice to stupid tweenagers who thought books like *Twilight* and *Hunger Games* were actual literature. These kids all looked down on me for having to work. *Wait until you want to go to college, wiseass,* I would think when they giggled and pointed at me lugging stacks of unshelved books.

Wait until your parents get on your case about logging in those volunteer hours. Who'll be the joke butt then?

"How'd you like my crapesthetic?" she asked.

"Funny, " I said. "Real effin funny."

"What're you doin'?" I could hear country music in the background, and the trapped room sound of drunken laughter. "S'up?"

"Working." I said. "Where the ef are you?"

"Drinking." She laughed. "I'm at the Wine Deck. I have Bradley in my sights. He is soooo hot. Okay if I give him a hummer?"

"FU, H8er, " I said in a tiny voice.

I wasn't angry, exactly. And I didn't exactly believe her. It sure didn't sound like she was at the Deck. No airboat roars, no osprey screams. Maybe she was just goofing on me. Still, she could be mean.

"Oooooh, is the little ex-virgin girl jealous? Well, let those deep feelings feed your work, Heller. And while you're at the book depository, get yourself some Plath. You need to bone up on your she-bitches."

With a short bark of laughter, she hung up.

At the tail end of my shift, I roamed around in the poetry aisle until I found a few volumes by Sylvia Plath. I opened a slim book called *Ariel*. Nice title, I liked the sound of it: short, strong, spirited, female but not fem.

Flipping through the pages I caught fragments of phrases, lines that seemed to jump out at me and singe my eyeballs. I stopped when I got to a poem called "Thalidomide." OMG, it ripped my lungs out! After I read it, I could hardly breathe. Then I scanned "Death & Co." SMD! I read the lines over and over, my pulse quickening, my heart surging uncontrollably. That poem did something to me. Something about how there were two, and then the dead bell. The dead bell!

I closed the book with great reluctance. It felt like the world around me had suddenly transformed, like in a fairy tale. Plath was a voice from beyond. A fairy godmother, a sprite, a she-goddess. And reading her work, it was like the poet was speaking directly to me. I could hear the drumbeat of her vicious words reverberating in my head. Her lines rang like a funeral bell. So true, so true.

Without even thinking about it, I tucked the book in my armpit and walked quickly to the break room. I pulled out my locker basket and stuffed the book into my backpack. Sylvia Plath was talking to me. I had to listen. I had to own her words. Consume them. Take them inside me. Right that minute.

Outside, I headed for the metallic green roof of the bus shelter on Main Street. Then I pulled out the book again and stood there, all alone in the warm, slowly encroaching darkness, reading. My eyes darted from poem to poem as I inhaled Plath's tumult of rage. If I'd formerly lived in Nerdvana, Plath had taken up residence in Ragevana. Fascinated, I allowed myself to be sucked down into her world. I liked it there. I *really* liked it. Wow.

I ended up waiting for a long time for a bus to show up. ("Nobody takes the bus in this town except for illegal immigrants, bean-eaters without driver's licenses," is how H8er sums up our local public transportation.) I might have stood on the corner for hours, I didn't care. I read like I was ravenous, eating up all that spicy emotion, the red hot dish of vitriol, the cold sweet dessert of revenge. I stood there on the curb, consuming the poet's rich, hate-fueled words until they filled me like a meal.

I could have called Mom to pick me up, but I didn't want to. She still wasn't speaking to me and the keys to the Land Rover had not been offered since we'd had our fight. I was hoping for a treaty by the weekend so H8er and I would have wheels, but I wasn't too sure Mom would forgive me by then. Whatever.

If Trixie hadn't pulled up in her brand new Indigo Blue Jaguar XF convertible, I might have been there all night. Entranced by Plath's poetry, my heart and mind in sync, the cells filling with a strange new sensation.

"Hello, darling. May I be of service?"

I swam out of my Plath reverie with a nightmarish confusion bordering on psychosis. I had been torn out of the whorling center of a rip-current of indignant wrath. But when I realized the interruption was coming from my fave neighbor, I slipped the book into my backpack and stepped off the curb.

"Lift home, darling? I'm on my way, climb aboard," Trixie offered.

She was heavily made up and perfectly done up, as always. Royal blue Ralph Lauren Matte jersey dress with the faux-wrap skirt, and classic Lauren Pumps with the Amelie Pointed Toe, topped off with an Italian flex-style Omega Choker and an armload of multi-strand bangle bracelets in silver and gold.

I tossed my backpack in back and slid into the passenger seat, marveling at the smooth rosewood trim on the dash and the impressive surround sound of her CD player. Elton was blasting. With Trixie, Elton was often blasting.

"What in god's name were you reading, hon? You had your

face sealed to the pages like you were French-kissing them," she teased.

Her grin was contagious. I had to laugh, too.

I want you to understand this. Trixie is the happiest person I've ever met. And I know why that is. Because she's on her way to someplace better. Some*one* better. Despite the odds, she's been able to march steadfastly past all those dumb, useless limits society, genetics, family and church set in our way. And she's left a lot of the BS behind her on the way to becoming someone else. Oh yeah, there's a lot more shit up ahead, of course there is. And she's not all the way there yet. But she's still on the move. Who will that new someone be? Who knows? Trixie's making herself up as she goes along.

But I didn't know that about her last April. I just knew that I liked her.

"Sylvia Plath, the poet. Ever read her?"

Trixie turned down "Candle in the Wind" and said, "I read *The Bell Jar* in high school. Back in the Dark Ages. Superior stuff, Aimee. Plath captures so beautifully the sad desperation of being a young person unable to keep up with expectations. I should reread that book. One of these days," she said wistfully.

Trixie was very busy. She ran an erotic ebook publishing company out of her home, played tennis and golf avidly, and had an active social life.

I made a mental note to get *The Bell Jar*.

"Speaking of high expectations, how's that mother of yours doing? Has she forgiven you for not getting into *her* priority schools?"

Trixie snorted and rolled her eyes. Her false lashes were thick as little Hitler mustaches.

I said, "She still thinks I'll get in somewhere I've been wait listed. But now she's distracted, so she's been on my case a little less."

Trixie nodded sympathetically. "Must be another new beau, right?"

I shrugged, like *You know Mom.*

Trixie and Mom maintained a polite and neighborly détente, but both were openly hostile to me about the other. Mom resented Trixie's gender bending, her blatant outsiderness, while Trixie told me my mom was phony, prefeminist, and elitist. Nothing I hadn't figured out on my own. I always enjoyed being around Trixie, but I could see why she irritated Mom. She was a man dressed exceedingly well in women's finery, and now she had what looked like a perfect set of B cups. Maybe C. Plus, her business was successful and she was rich.

"Mom's going out with a professor. From Hope Shore College. A writing teacher."

Trixie gasped dramatically. "She is *not!* That's trespassing. Invasion of your personal boundaries! Is he *your* professor?"

I shrugged. "Maybe I'll change my major to urban studies. Then transfer out after freshman year."

"To the University of Alaska, I hope." Trixie heaved a huge sigh. Her chest rose and fell. Just like a real one. "Child, the best thing you can do for yourself is move out of that house. I had to take my life into my own hands too, when I was not much older than you are now."

She nodded to herself, probably remembering the Trixie-Tomas wars of her adolescence. Hispanic families can be even less cool about LGBT issues than other parents. Although my mom is a total hard-ass on the entire subject. *Total* hard-ass. If anyone even smells gay, she sniffs, nose in the air, then frowns her deep and abiding disapproval.

"How can you decide who you are, darling, if someone else is always telling you who you aren't?" She switched off the music and powered down our windows. The sea air was crisp, salty. Our hair whipped even faster around our heads. "Is this too much for you, darling?"

"No. I love a good hard wind."

"Good for you, Aimee. Because throughout your life, you can bet you'll find yourself lost in a *lot* of hard winds."

She was being poetic, so I didn't say anything.

"My two cents, for what they're worth? You want some words of wisdom from the fairy next door?"

I laughed, and Trixie patted my shoulder with her big, heavily ringed, perfectly manicured hand. "I love you, darling. Ever since you were a wee little girl, so beautiful, so sweet. I adore you, dearest, you know that, right? So please, take my advice as coming from Aunt Trix, from a person who cares. Okay?"

I nodded. We were passing through the guard gate and I was losing interest. I'd had enough advice from well-intentioned adults to last me a lifetime. What I needed most at this point was to learn how to listen to myself.

"Tell that mother of yours what you want from her. What you want for yourself. Put those feelings into words, Aimee. Don't hold back. And stop being the perfect daughter. It's not good for you. Ultimately, you have to be a little bit nasty to become a whole person."

There was something nasty about Trixie, that was true. The shadow of a beard under the heavy layer of foundation she always wore on her face. The dark hair furring her arms.

Her broad muscular shoulders and commanding voice. But she was so chic too. Feminine and classy in her dress, her choice of words. And a nice person. A caring person.

"I don't know what I want, though," I admitted to her. Had no fucking idea, actually.

"Do you want your mom sleeping with your college professor?"

I shook my head. "Course not. But really, is it my business who she's with?"

"In this particular instance it is."

We pulled into her narrow brick driveway. She turned off the engine but left the top down, the windows open. The cool evening air felt good on my skin. We sat in the car talking in the soft darkness. I could smell the sweet magnolia tree in full bloom on Trixie's front lawn.

She was being so supportive, and that was like totally nice of her. I couldn't disagree with her. She was totally right about everything she was saying.

Still, it was Plath's words that rushed through my head as I thanked my neighbor for the ride home and the good talk. It was Plath's rage that fired up my heart as I walked next door, my backpack heavy on my shoulder. Why, I'm not sure. Maybe I *wanted* to be enraged, maybe it just *felt* good.

Whatever the reason, that was how I felt. Pissed at the world, and happy about that.

And the feeling only got stronger. Which, as you know, is why we are where we are today. Like Plath said, somebody was done for.

Ten: FTW

IT WAS H8ER'S idea to break into Trixie's house and steal some liquor. Not mine. BH, I would *never* have dreamed of doing something like that. I mean, a library book was one thing. My mom's half-drunk wine and half-forgotten champagne, like who cared? But to actually trespass on someone else's property, invade their house and nab some of their stuff? No way.

"No way," I said to H8er when she first brought it up. "No freaking way."

"Pussy," she responded.

As always, this pissed me off and, at the same time, somehow egged me on. H8er was always encouraging me to man up. It was exasperating.

I felt a brief stab of hate for my BFF. Then I just shrugged her off.

Like a half hour later, she brought it up again. We were hanging in the kitchen, drinking Coke Zeros. She was smoking a doobie she'd bought from some guy at the bus station. It smelled fried, and the rolling paper was all greasy, so I wasn't partaking. Ew. Who knew where that joint had been?

Earlier, when she'd bugged me about breaking into my mom's stash, I'd had to lie and say I didn't know where the key to the wine closet was. Truth was, I wasn't up for filching any of the super-expensive bottles in my mom's Sonoma Wine Cabinet because I was already in the shit with her. I wasn't going to unlock the off-white weathered wood door and grab a three hundred dollar grand cru, it was just too risky and totally not worth it. Forget it. Besides, I already had the hazy beginnings of a headache. I felt like shit. My sleep had been getting worse and worse so I felt kind of vulnerable.

But H8er was jonesing for a drink. We were going out later, much later, with Bradley, and she didn't want to wait until he got off work at midnight to get drunk.

"Me want booze," she whined. "Come on, Heller. Don't be a prissy-bitch-snob. It's fucking Friday night and I'm hungry, thirsty, pissy and bored. Mostly thirsty."

Mostly pissy, I wanted to say. But I didn't. Eventually, I did give in to her regarding Trixie's. Mainly because I doubted she'd have the prowler skills to get inside the house.

"SMD, H8er," I said finally. "So go ahead and do it then. I'll come with for moral support. I'll even stand guard, if you want. But I'm not going in with you. And if the cops or anybody else show up, I'm out of there. I'll flat out deny I even know you."

I meant it, too.

H8er laughed. "Suit yourself, faggot. I'm goin' in. And I might not let you have any of my bodacious haul, either."

The HuffPo headline I liked best that day was: *Supersizing Makes Consumers Feel More Important, Study Says.* Yeah, okay, Study: I got no argument witchoo. Gimme more, I feel better about my fat self. Right? In reality, it's us consumers who are the victims of global-scale, ego-bloating, obesity-creating advertising campaigns. We can't help it if we feel like we deserve the best of everything and more of it than any one person could ever really need. It isn't our fault, we've been brainwashed from birth.

So what if H8er wanted in to someone else's place, someone else's liquor supply? So she wanted to supersize her high, so what? This here's America, goddam it! Just do it, right?

Right.

I went out front to check. The Jag wasn't in the driveway. Trixie usually stayed in Fort Lauderdale at her boyfriend's on Friday nights, so they could party with their friends in Wilton Manors. Which is like gay central. I figured she'd be back on Saturday to work on her lush yard. She did all the lawn work herself. The backyard was like a botanical garden.

"Don't mess up her plants," I warned H8er as we tiptoed across my lawn toward Trixie's. "Or her cats. She'd be more upset about that than about you taking her stuff."

I felt protective of Trixie, but there was no controlling H8er. Once she got an idea in her head, she went for it. I could have stayed home, but I was curious. I wasn't sure how she expected to break in. She hadn't asked to borrow so much as a hammer.

We hurried up the winding brick walkway in the dark and ducked onto Trixie's front porch. A full arbor of lovely red- and purple-flowered bougainvillea bushes hid us from the street. Which was deserted anyway. Palm Ridge Hills is dead by mid-April, which is when all the snowbirds go back up north. Since most of the rest of the residents are like senior citizens, everyone is tucked into their twin beds and asleep by eight. No lights blazing in any of the houses. Few cars zipping in and out of driveways. Even on weekend nights. Which is kind of creepy.

"What's that phat smell?" H8er whispered.

I sniffed the air. "Night blooming jasmine," I told her. "That massive vine over there."

She looked at where I was pointing, a tumble of greenery on the far end of the front porch. Tiny white flowers sparkled in the moonlight. She stood there for a moment, still sniffing the air. "Someone should bottle that aroma. Sell it. Make a mint."

"Someone already has," I whispered. "BTW, how you getting in? You're not gonna try breaking a window, are you? Those are hurricane-proof panes, you'll need like a crowbar."

"Duh," she said in a normal voice.

She bent down to lift up the stubbly welcome mat. It was dark green with a big yellow pineapple on it. In my neighborhood, everyone had welcome pineapples on display—on mats, flags and banners, sitting atop brass lamp posts and carved into the wood of front gates—but this was another example of false advertising. Nobody was the least bit friendly or welcoming in Palm Ridge Hills.

Except for Trixie. And here we were, B&E-ing her.

H8er peeled back the corner of the mat and there it was. The front door key. Lying there on the crackled Chicago bricks, like it had been waiting for us.

I kind of startled and H8er said, "Relax, Heller. You're the one who told me she left it under here. All this is *your* fault." She laughed when I slapped my head. "See, I've got a good memory, Heller. Especially for fucking salient details that might come in handy at a later date."

I backed away. "You're on your own, Sturter. I'm waiting over there, by the ficus hedge."

I turned around and scurried off. I wanted nothing to do with the rest of this little escapade. I felt guilty enough. Me and my big mouth.

By the time I looked back, I couldn't see H8er anywhere.

The front door was closed, Trixie's house dark and still.

My heart pounded in my ears. The adrenaline rush was really kind of cool. But soon enough I got bored. I contemplated sneaking up to the house and spying in the windows. But I was too chickenshit. So I just stood there, thinking about what a nice person Trixie was, and how she'd always been kind to me.

After what seemed like an intolerably long wait, I heard the slam of Trixie's front door. H8er jogged up, panting and giggling.

"OMG, what a trip! You should see all the shit that guy has to go through to make himself a girl. His bedroom is like a movie set, like a makeup and costume trailer or something. Wigs on like bald heads, plastic falsies, weird straps for whatever—"

"Shut the fuck up," I said. "Tell me you didn't touch anything when you were snooping around in there. Cuz I could get blamed for this, you know."

"Calm down, sissy. Everything's totally copacetic."

She pushed by me and headed for my house, her arms full of loot.

Back in my kitchen, H8er showed me what she'd stolen from Trixie's. A bottle of Stoli Hot; two unopened bottles of what looked like very expensive European wine (both reds, so they might as well have had migraine warning labels directed at me personally); a tin of River Beluga caviar ("I always wanted to try this black egg shit," H8er said when I laughed at it); and a thick wad of cash. Wrapped with rubber bands.

The cash pissed me off.

"What the fuck, H8er," I said.

"For me, to entertain myself while you're off somewhere

fucking Bradley," she explained with a shrug. When I started to protest, she said, "Unless you want a ménage a twat?" I said nothing. "I thought not. So calm the fuck down, man. Second time is always better. You'll enjoy it this time. Meanwhile, I'll have nothing to do."

This seemed unlikely, but I knew how she felt. I was often third wheel with my mom and her men and it was no fun, no fun at all.

H8er stuffed the cash in the hip pocket of my mom's best leather-look GUESS Power Skinny jeans. The pants looked effing great on her, but I was keeping my fingers crossed she didn't ruin them. So far, Mom hadn't mentioned her missing clothes. I mean, she has a room full of the newest fashions and her wardrobe's as diverse as it is copious, so I was hoping maybe the ruined velvet pants would go unnoticed for a while. But I was pretty sure that, eventually, our clothes thieving would catch up to us.

And now there was a home invasion that could so easily be pinned on us. On *me*. After all, I was the one who took care of Trixie's plants and two sweet, overweight house cats whenever she went out of town for publishing conventions. I had access. H8er was an unknown, but I wasn't.

I could now add paranoia to my list of headaches. And my insomnia wasn't going to cure itself this weekend. Not unless I drank myself into a stupor. Again. As George Orwell once said (supposedly): "A man takes to drink because he is a failure, and then fails all the more because he drinks."

Change the "he" to a "she" and you have Aimee Heller, AH. Failure and drinking. Worked for me.

H8er opened Mom's handcrafted Tree Branch display cabinet with reeded glass doors. She studied the shelves.

Of course she then selected my mom's absolute *best* wine glasses, Bordeaux glasses in handblown crystal from Tiffany's. Practically prancing, she popped opened one of the reds, a 2007 Chambolle-Musigny Bonnes-Mares Burgundy, and poured.

The wine smelled old, funky. It was like room temperature, too warm for my taste. When I gagged a little on my first sip, H8er snorted.

"You choke that down, doofus. This bottle is worth like more than Bradley's shitbox car," she snickered.

"How do you know what he drives?"

"How do you think?" She sneered, then chugged her wine. "Like all guys, he's randy for candy. Teenage candy. Like you. Or me, he doesn't care." She poured herself more wine. "Do you?"

I did and I didn't. Maybe I wasn't sure what I felt. I sort of wanted her to take him off my hands because he seemed way too much for me to handle. An adult male with sexual needs I knew nothing about. I had barely kissed guys my own age, and now I was fucking a grownup? I shrugged, sipped the nasty wine.

"Like a boss, Heller. You're learning. Good for you."

I wasn't sure what she meant.

"A lousy C.E. is just that, *casual* encounter, right? Sex for sex, fun for fun. But look at Heller Senior. All about guys. That's how she lives, what she fucking lives for. In any account of your mom's life, the men would receive top billing. So what I'm saying is, good for you, Heller. You're not her."

This flattered me. I felt a supersizing going on. Good for me? Hellz yeah. It was what I wanted more than anything, when I thought about it. To live for myself, not somebody else. To be Aimee Heller, not Marlene Heller.

"Now we just gotta work on you manning up," H8er said with a half-smile.

We were sitting across from one another at the kitchen island. Slumping on our elbows, slopped over all lazy on the black and white bar stools. I looked directly into my friend's pale face. Which was healing nicely, the bruised eye socket yellowing now, her small straight nose perfect as before. I stared into her wide eyes and watched, fascinated, as the iris faded from lilac to a soft gray.

"Your eyes? What color would you say they are?" I asked. Maybe I was higher than I thought.

"I wouldn't say. I'd say, who gives a fuck? Don't go gay on me, Heller."

"Funny. But really, sometimes your eyes look blue, sometimes—"

The land line rang and we both jumped a little in our seats.

"FTW," H8er said. "Who's calling on the dinosaur phone? Moms?"

"Must be a salesperson. Or some dipshit reminding me to vote in the November election. First one I'll finally be old enough to vote in. Too bad I don't give two shits." I slid off my stool and crossed the room to the wall phone. "Or it could be my grandfather. He won't call us on our cells. Says it's too easy for the government to listen in."

I snorted, but just before I picked up the receiver H8er said, "He has a point there."

"Agnes?" Grampy said.

"No. It's me, Aimee."

I tried for a while to explain that Marlene was out and

I was her daughter, his granddaughter, but Grampy wasn't having any of it. H8er laughed her butt off and drank like a ton of the Burgundy by herself while I wrangled with my grandfather. Finally, he resigned himself to something, I'm not sure what, and I thought I was getting somewhere with him at last.

"Mom, I mean Marlene, won't be home tonight. Do you want us to come visit on Sunday, Grampy?"

"Listen, girl, you tell Agnes that I'm ready for target practice. I've been waiting for you to bring her out here so we can have some gun fun."

"*Gun fun?* Okay, Grampy, but this isn't Agnes, it's me, Aimee. I'm the one that wants to practice shooting with you—"

H8er jumped up and snatched the receiver out of my hand.

"Hi," she said in a cheery voice. "This is Agnes."

She stepped back when I reached for the phone, avoiding my outstretched hand. She turned her back to me and hunched over, continuing the conversation, ignoring me when I bent down to catch her eye, waving away my strained facial commands. *Shit.*

"Uh-huh," she said to my grandfather a few times. And, "Oh, sure. Sure."

Once again, I gave in, let her do what she'd decided to do. That was another thing about H8er: she almost always got her way. It was easier to just let H8er do what she had a mind to do. H8er would be H8er. All I could do was hope that I wasn't going to end up in even deeper shit than I was already in.

You know how well *that* turned out for me.

When she sauntered out of the kitchen, I was hanging in the

living room, lying on my side on the couch. I'd texted Bradley and he was sexting back. I was laughing but, really, it was sort of grossing me out. All that illiterate nonsense about how we would make each other come was really turning me off.

"We have a date with the NRA for any afternoon next week. Target practice. He says he'll provide guns and ammo. Am I supposed to believe he has all the firearms he claims he has?"

I shrugged. "What exactly did he tell you he has?"

I set my iPhone on the Paper Plane Coffee Table by Lorraine Brennan and sat up. H8er sank onto the plushy cushion beside me, propping her dirty feet on the stark white table. Mom would have a shit fit if she saw. I kind of cringed, said nothing.

"A Beretta M9. A .300 magnum rifle, a 12-gauge shotgun, a .30.30 Winchester lever-action carbine. A Remington 870 12-gauge shotgun. A Smith & Wesson Model 29 .44 Magnum— for shooting bears, he says. A .45 caliber Glock. A .22 caliber pistol. A Sig Sauer P226 9mm police weapon. An AK-47 with 7.62 millimeter bullets and a 75-round drum magazine." She paused. "There's more, but that's all I remember him saying."

I giggled. "You're shitting me."

"I shit you not, Heller. I'm dead-ass serious."

My phone beeped and H8er picked it up, examining the Instagram with a clinical eye. "Subaverage size and diameter, just as I remember it," she said. "You gonna hit it with this thang, girlfriend?"

I peeked over her shoulder. "Ew. I sure don't remember it looking like that. Ick." I shuddered. "Let's uninvite him tonight. I'm suddenly not so interested in experiencing a second time with that guy."

H8er shrugged. "Suit yourself. I'll go out with him. I want to suck him off. It'll get rid of the taste of that putrid caviar."

She bared her teeth to show me the grayish eggs stuck between her front teeth. "Can I borrow your toothbrush?" she asked.

Eleven: Stoli Hot

HERE'S THE RECIPE for a Stoli Hot Shot Hangover Cure: two parts Stoli Hot (premium Russian vodka flavored with spicy peppers), four parts tomato juice; shake with shaved ice, garnish with a jalapeno pepper.

If you have caviar for breakfast after the first Hot Shot, serve it with crusty white toast. Crème fraîche is optional.

Although nothing beats a hangover like getting an IV installed. Especially an IV hand-administered by a physician on call for booze-fueled tourists on a bad run in Vegas. But the Stoli Hot Shot Hangover Cure works pretty well for those next-day post-party ailments.

I ought to know. I tried the spicy concoction myself and my hangover like totally went away.

When Bradley arrived after midnight on that Friday night, I ran upstairs and let H8er go to the door. We'd been watching her fave film, *The Big Lebowski*. I didn't quite understand her love for the movie, it was so retro, but I did expect to have a few flashback bowling dreams.

I stretched out on my bed and tried to sleep. I could hear them talking downstairs, like I didn't exist. I heard laughing, glasses clinking. Somebody put the Marilyn Manson CD on. Somebody changed it to Tom Petty.

When the CD ended, I was still awake. I would have been woken up anyway by H8er's deep throated, raging bear growls, her long-winded moans. They were really going at it.

My door was closed and my bedroom cool, dark, still. Downstairs, somebody laughed and I heard what sounded like someone sucking a milkshake through a thin straw. I put my pillow over my head. I felt weird, kind of like a ghost. Definitely like a social reject.

Still, I was glad it wasn't me having sex with a horny twenty-something. Plus, I had a really bad headache. One glass of the stolen vino and my head throbbed like a fresh bruise.

The next morning when I wandered downstairs, Bradley was sitting at the kitchen island with a Stoli Hot Shot. He was shirtless, sun-bronzed and toned like a Banana Republic model.

"Hey, gorgeous," he said. "I made breakfast."

Make yourself at home, why don't you, was what I thought. But I said nothing. The situation was like totally awkward. Plus, he was like totally stunningly buff.

He recited the recipe while mixing me a drink. Stoli Hot Shot. Simple, but with an undeniable excellence. "And this shit works like a charm. Head, stomach, all like new. You watch, babe."

Babe. Ick.

He went on and on about hangovers and drink cures while I sat there like a dumb numb lump. I was speechless. What was I going to do, tell him to leave? The idea of imbibing an alcoholic beverage at eleven a.m. only added to my uneasiness, but when he set the glass in front of me I didn't know what to say. It didn't look half bad. A cute little hot pepper floating in a sea of red. It actually looked kind of adorable. So I took a sip.

Yum. The thing was good. Spicy. Not at all boozy. Tasted like an energized V8.

I liked it.

"Thanks," I mumbled.

He laughed. "Your house. Your Stoli," he said.

Right. But not, as it turned out, my boyfriend.

"You're so shy this morning. I can't keep up with your mood swings, babe."

Huh? I stood there sipping my drink. When I looked over, he was grinning at me. Shit, his teeth were white. Like starched sheets on a golden beach.

I shrugged. "Maybe I'm not so good with alcohol."

He laughed. "You'll get better. The way you drink, you'll be a pro in no time."

He paused and stared at me while I tried to figure out whether he meant that as a compliment.

"You were doing okay last night. More than okay."

How would *he* know? I focused on the drink. Extremely yum.

He came and stood beside me, so close I could smell the leftover weed smoke, beer, and real manly man sweat. I liked his smell so I didn't pull away. That must have been the wrong move because he reached over and grabbed my face with both hands, pressed it against his warm hairless chest. Wrapped his nicely muscled arms around me, hugging me to him.

I was so shocked I couldn't move. But my legs trembled. I needed to sit down. I tried to calm myself by listening to the steady beat of his heart. Blub, blub. Kind of comforting in a primitive animal kind of way.

Still, how awkward. He fucks me, takes the V. Then fucks my BFF. In my house, no less. Now, less than twelve hours later, he's coming on to me again?

Men are so weird. Like a different breed of animal. One lacking any sense of loyalty.

He lifted my chin up so I had to look into those sea-glass eyes of his. He was so good looking. What a waste.

He whispered, "I could really *like* you, kid."

His breath smelled pretty bad. Like menthol and canned tomatoes.

I kind of pushed him away. WTF was he doing? "Well, tell that to the judge. I'm only seventeen."

I sank onto a bar stool and worked on my drink, not looking at him.

After about a minute of weird-vibed silence, he said, "Um, okay, have it your way, dude. Thanks for the good time."

He let himself out. His shitbox car sounded like a cheap blender when he started it up.

What a loser.

Sun splashed around the kitchen, lighting here and there on a midget hot pepper, a bamboo cutting board, a quilted oven mitt, a copper pot. A sweet breeze blew in the screen door that led out to the garage, bringing the aroma of spring, fresh lawn clippings, and Trixie's magnolia blossoms. A couple of lusty mocking birds were singing their little hearts out, imitating all their fave species, defending their bushes or seeking willing mates.

In a sort of comfortable torpor, I sat there working my Stoli Hot Shot until I was sucking ice. Then I got up and made myself another one. With a generous pile of caviar on toast. And a side of Kendall Farms All-Natural Crème Fraîche.

My headache was gone.

So was H8er.

Twelve: Like a Boss

H8ER WENT MISSING after that. In fact, she was absent from my life for more than a month. Except for one phone call, on April 20th. That ought to give you a good solid clue: *April 20th*. Like 4:20? Typical H8er, right?

Just before she called, I'd run a psychotic number of laps on the outdoor track. The late afternoon air was thick with early summer humidity and I was drenched in lazy sweat. Coach Meyer gave me the thumbs up, sent me inside to hit the showers.

My training had been solid lately and I'd done pretty well (for a change) at the all high schools meet held in Winter Haven over the weekend. I didn't place, but I didn't humiliate myself either. Coach Meyer said he was pleased with my performance. I'm not sure what he saw in me because I wasn't one of his star runners, but maybe he liked the way I just hung in there, even when the going got tough. He'd begun saying I should continue to train, even though HSC didn't have a girls' track team.

I wasn't clear on whether I would keep at it, but I was open to the idea. Running is totally mindless but it takes focus. So it provides a nice break from thinking about how shitty your life is.

At my locker, I toweled off and checked my phone. I was majorly surprised to see that H8er had called. No message, though.

Before I could strip off my Nike Boyshorts, my phone rang and I picked up. She didn't explain where she'd been hiding or why. She just said, "Long live Eric and Dylan."

"Who?" I asked. "Hey, aren't you going out with Bradley anymore?"

I made my voice hard, kind of snotty. I wasn't annoyed at her over losing him, I was mostly relieved. But I didn't appreciate the fact that she'd dumped me and taken up with the guy. I mean, weren't we supposed to be cooler than that? Couldn't she still hang with me even though she was fucking my sort of ex-boyfriend?

I didn't say any of this to her.

"Who?" she said. "Oh, him. He's history. I'm referring to the Columbine boyz, Heller. Think about it. Except for you, world's biggest nerd with her head permanently up her A-grade ass, *everyone* is thinking about Eric and Dylan today."

"Why?"

"SMD, I can't fucking *believe* you're a National Merit Scholar, Heller," she groaned. "*Because*, you big tard, today is the thirteenth anniversary of the Columbine school shooting. Meaning my personal heroes have been gone for thirteen full years. And nobody, but *nobody*, has been able to outdo them. In all this time." She sniffed. "And not for lack of trying, either. There are like these school shootings practically every month. Lame ones. Copycat massacres that aren't. Not like Dylan and Eric, man. Those guys had it *down*."

"There was the guy in Norway," I said. "He killed more than seventy people."

"He's an *adult*, Heller. And he had political reasons for shooting all those camp kids." She paused. "It wasn't *random*.

116

As far as the random teen violence record goes, Harris and Klebold absolutely fucking rule."

What about that guy at Virginia Tech, I was thinking. But I didn't want to argue about it. Like who cared who was the worst of the lot? They were all effed-up creeps. I had no interest in them or their despicable crimes.

"Think about it, Heller. Just imagine if two *girls* masterminded a monster school shooting! Imagine how much attention *all* troubled girls would receive after that! Nobody would call chicks *pussies* anymore. They wouldn't dare, not if we pulled off a Columbine."

"We? What do you mean, *we?*" I said, tempted to hang up. WTF was she talking about?

"We, Heller. As in, you and me. As in, us creating a way to bring attention to the truth. The truth being that girls are angry, too. We hate, and we're filled with rage about the world around us. Like we have rights, too. The right to be violent. The right to act out when we can't take the shit piling up anymore."

She was talking crazy. I instantly realized that I hadn't missed her at all while she'd been incommunicado. In fact, I'd liked my life without her in it.

"Why exactly are you calling me, Skitchen?" I tried to make my voice sound impersonal, businesslike. "I'm busy."

She disconnected. I called her back and went straight to voice message.

"Leave me the fuck alone, H8er," I said to her message machine. I stated it as clearly and meanly as possible. "I have a life without you and I'm liking it that way."

Then there were more weeks of nothing but silence between us.

In retrospect, those weeks without H8er were good ones. High school was less of a grind, mostly because the pressure had eased. No more need to score those perfect grades for college admission. Too late for that. So all I did was my homework. Instead of staying up half the night overdoing it. Mom wasn't on my case either. She was so into her new love affair she hardly seemed to notice what I was up to.

My college classes were good, too. I especially enjoyed Professor Whitehead's Intro to Literature. The other students seemed totally apathetic, distracted in class, relying on CliffsNotes, ClassicNotes, shit like that. They used shortcuts for like *everything*. I'd hear them between classes, asking each other who they could pay to write their papers for them. Which was sort of appalling. Why shell out six figures to attend a private college, then pay more money for somebody else to do your schoolwork for you? I didn't get them, these rich kids who didn't care about learning anything. But I did like the lit class. Yeats, Hawthorne, Fitzgerald, Nabokov, Flannery O'Connor; what's not to like?

My afterschool life started shaping up, too. Like I already told you, track was going well. The library job wasn't, I hated my volunteer serf role, and Mom shocked me by finally agreeing to let me quit. At the end of April, I said my goodbyes to the circulation desk with a huge sigh of relief. (As H8er would have said, *No more Heller nigga to kick around anymore.*)

In early May, the *Sounder* published my student essay on the influence of political correctness on duplicity in the culture (*If we can't call a spade a spade anymore, what should we call a heart?* I asked the paper's mostly conservative and morally constipated readership.) We got a ton of instant flak on the piece and the paper's managing editor was thrilled. He called me to report that his advertisers loved the brouhaha. I guess when a lot of offended townspeople sent in steaming hot letters to the editor, then other readers emailed to say what hypocritical assholes their neighbors were, and the silly tussle in print boosted readership. At least for a few weeks. I enjoyed my infamy for like a minute before everybody forgot and moved on to proper hedge height and the controversy over allowing neon in signs for downtown businesses.

Words are like that. They blow up, but the explosion doesn't destroy anything. Actions, though, make a different kind of impact. One the world won't forgive. Or forget. But I wasn't thinking about it that way. Not yet.

Two other good things happened in May: Bitsy and I resumed our friendship, and me and my mom kind of bonded, which was cool.

One night after dinner I was up in my room doing homework when the doorbell rang. Mom called up, "I'll get it. Marc is dropping off my handbag. I left it in his car last night."

I didn't roll my eyes, slam my door, say under my breath, *Now I'll have to listen to those two sucking face all night.* I just yelled down to her, "'kay, Moms."

But it wasn't my mom's lover. It was Bitsy.

I froze in my desk chair when I recognized her laugh. Mom called up, "Your friend's here, Aimee."

While Bitsy bounded up the stairs to my room, I sat there like a weirdo, freaking. It had been so long since she'd come over, I wasn't sure how to feel. Happy to see her? Annoyed she'd stayed away?

We smiled tentatively at one another. "Hey," I said,

shutting my physics text and pushing it toward the book pile that crowded my desk. "S'up?"

I wanted to be casual and uncaring, but that wasn't what I was feeling. To my own surprise, I jumped up and ran over, throwing my arms around her tiny waist and squeezing my long lost pal in a big bear hug. She hugged me back, giggling.

"I missed you, Bits," I said.

What a wussy thing to say. But there was a painful lump in my throat. I *had* missed her.

She patted my back gently. "Me too. Want to go get ice cream at Bender's?"

"Sure, love to," I said. And meant it.

Even though it was a school night, Mom let me go. Maybe because she was waiting for Professor Dimitri to come by and she wanted the privacy. Maybe because she knew I needed time with my ex-BFF. Whatever her reasons, she didn't give me a curfew, so Bitsy and I took advantage of that.

We drove straight to the beach and parked in the public lot facing the ocean, which was flat as an infinity pool. We kept on talking the whole time about the phony assholes at Central, teachers who were still major pains even though it was too late for them to change us, we were *out of there*, and our plans for the fall. Bitsy said she was scared about moving to Ithaca, and my jealousy diminished a little. She might be valedictorian and all-Ivy, but she still had crippling social issues. Just like I did.

We got started on the upcoming senior prom. Neither of us had been invited, so we made lame jokes about the one we'd attended together. Bitsy didn't drink alcohol and I hadn't started yet when we doubled to last year's prom. We went with a couple of Irish kids from the soccer team. God only knows why they'd asked us to go. Maybe because we were social unknowns, so we wouldn't expect much from them.

We didn't get much either.

"Being his date was like getting a mercy fuck, but without the sex," Bitsy recalled. "I mean, Jerry was so blotto, he couldn't even stand up, never mind get *it* up. Not that I wanted him to. His teeth were like mossy. Ewwwww."

We both laughed, even though this was all very familiar territory. Our one adventure in high school high society had already been combed through obsessively many, many times since it had gone down.

"Irish Catholics don't want to have sex," I prognosticated. "Too dirty. A sin they'll have to lie about or confess. That's why they drink so much." So, was that *my* excuse? I didn't want to go there. I hadn't had a sip of alcohol in weeks, and this felt like an accomplishment. "Sean had a tongue like a gecko. It was like darting in and out, snatching at bugs on my tonsils. And so boozy, it made me drunk just having it in my mouth."

We snickered, pretending to gag. But the flood of memories from that night felt like a made-up story about some other girl. The me who went to that prom in my one-shoulder floor-length turquoise Atria gown with a short train (sexy, elegant, awkward), my long hair wound up into French braids, my hymen tight and proud, that was a different person than the girl I'd become. The Aimee sitting in an i-series convertible watching a bright yellow moon lift itself above the unfurling waves of the frothing sea, she was someone other than the girl Bitsy and I remembered. It was like the double-dating prom girl was Heidi, my mom's perfect daughter, the straight A student with a shining future. That girl was gone.

Whatever happened to Heidi? And what about Aimee? Who exactly *was* she?

I didn't want to go there either.

Bitsy revved the engine and backed out of the deserted lot.

"Prom weekend is coming up. Do you have plans?" she asked.

She didn't look over at me, but I heard her suck in her breath. She had taken a chance coming to visit me to patch up our friendship. Now she was taking another one.

We pulled up to a stop sign and waited. A1A was quiet, airbrushed, the coconut palms waving their fronds in a gentle offshore breeze.

Bitsy was admitting her loneliness. She wanted me to hang out with her and pretend we didn't care that we weren't invited to our senior prom. When I thought about it, I was grateful. I mean, I felt totally glad not to have to go through the archaic ritual again. Once was plenty. But Bitsy might have felt differently. I didn't ask.

"No plans," I told her.

So we made some. My house, a dumb romcom we'd both seen dozens of times, piles of junk food. Maybe a quick drive over to the Hyatt to spy on the stretch limos and dolled-up couples heading in or out of the ballroom.

Our plan settled, we drove downtown and parked in front of Bender's. We went into the cutesy little ma and pa shop with its half-dozen plastic tables and shiny posters of happy ice cream concoctions all over the bright pink walls. No line. We both ordered double waffle cones with almond crunchies. We sat there for like an hour, yakking and laughing. Most of the tension that had ruined things for us seemed to be gone. It felt like old times with us.

After that, we drove around aimlessly for a while, still catching up, before she dropped me off at my house.

Things on the home front were looking up, too. Mom was like majorly in love with Professor Dimitri, which I'm sure contributed to the improvement in our relationship. She'd kind of backed off my case and stopped with the constant nagging about grades and my résumé, so that helped as well. She gave me my own set of keys to the Land Rover and we divvied up the driving. Without a word of explanation, she totally dropped the idea of going to Virginia (or anywhere else) to demand that the college admission boards overthrow my wait list status and invite me to attend. So that particular guillotine of humiliation had been removed from above my skinny neck, thank god.

It appeared that Mom had adjusted to the idea of me matriculating to Hope Shore College in the fall. She didn't refer to it as the school for nitwits anymore. Which it was. Apparently, Professor Dimitri had convinced her that the academics were second only to Harvard, the HSC English department one of the best in the country. What a bullshit artist. But, so what? In fact, I was glad he was full of crapesthetics. Now Mom was totally off my ass about college.

So things were improving all around. Life wasn't anything to get high over, of course, my life was still wack as shit. But I felt better than I had in like four years. Maybe longer. I was sleeping better, and I hadn't had a super bad headache in weeks.

The migraine cure had come from Mom back in April. She'd heard me wandering around the house in the middle of the night and got up to see what was wrong.

"Headache," I told her. "Can't sleep."

"Oh, honey. That bad?"

When I nodded, glum and in obvious pain, pacing around in the dark, unable to sit still or rest, she got upset.

"This is *bullshit*, Aimee. We'll go back to Dr. Digger. Get something stronger for you. Even though he says they're just tension headaches, you need *something* to help you through them. This is *unacceptable*. Plus, you've lost weight. I don't like where this is headed."

She sighed, exasperated. IMHO, Dr. Digger is an A-number-one a-hole, like most pediatricians. They treat older kids like babies and then resent it when you get pissed off and switch to another doctor. I had no faith in Dr. Digger. I held my head in my palms like it was a cut grapefruit.

Mom came over and hugged me. She had like tears in her eyes!

"I don't like to do this, sweetie, but I'm going to give you something. It's prescription, so I really shouldn't. But I just *hate* to see you like this."

"What is it?" I asked.

I mean, I would have taken anything at that point. Remember, this was when I was still alternating my hangovers with wildass benders with H8er, feeling either giddy or totally putrid. If Mom had handed me crank, I swear, I would have snorted it. If that's what you do with crystal meth, I'm not up on my street drugs. Too much time in Nerdvana.

"Ambien," she said. "I've got Prozac, Luvox, and Paxil on hand, but I think the Ambien will work in a pinch."

She went into her room to get me some.

Huh? Mom on meds? I was totally floored. She'd never mentioned taking stuff to control her moods. She hadn't ever talked about seeing a therapist, or even hinted that she was feeling depressed. And, to be honest, she'd *always* seemed like such a bitchy crab. *Heil Hitler,* was what I said under my breath while she bossed my whole life around. Whenever she fell for a guy, she'd become a little different, more dreamy, nicer. But she still acted all stern and controlling with me most of the time. After one of her affairs ended, the bitchiness factor increased. But, all this time, the idea that Moms suffered from depression had never entered my mind.

When she came back from her bathroom with an Ozeri Curva Artisan Double Wall Tumbler full of tap water and an innocuous looking, salmon-colored capsule, I asked her, "Since when, Moms?"

I swallowed the pill and she fiddled with my messy hair, moving stray strands into place. "Oh, I've been a fan of happy pills for *years,* Aim. I had a lot of, well, *problems,* after your father decided to stay with that whore-bitch wife of his. And then I had a touch of postpartum. After you were born."

"Really? Oh, wow. You never told me that," I said.

She sank down onto the couch and unbelted her white cashmere-blend Luxury Waffle Robe from Brooks Brothers. She was wearing her mannish, long-sleeved, Intimo Silk Pajama in ivory, and House of Fraser Just Sheepskin Wooly Slippers. She had to have been hot. All I had on was on an oversize tee-shirt in navy from Out of the Closet with white block lettering that said *Use Your Dorsal Lateral Prefrontal Cortex.* Geek humor.

I curled up next to Mom with my head in her lap, and she gently massaged my forehead and my temples while she talked. Her hands were cool, smooth, and smelled great. Like tea tree oil and lemon.

She said my dad was the love of her life and he'd promised to leave Berit, his wife, but then he didn't because the divorce would have cost him too much. He would have had to give up a lot since he was the one who'd cheated. I knew about this already, I'd heard it all before. But then she told me some new stuff. Like how she'd thought about getting an abortion but couldn't go through with it, she was already madly in love with me. Like how I was the best thing about her life and always had been. And like how, for a long time after Dads replaced her with an endless string of willing twenty-year-olds, she'd been wounded. Being a new mom and alone, she'd been completely overwhelmed. Most days she'd felt totally drained of her normal energy, and sad. Exhausted and deeply, deeply sad.

"Prozac saved my life, Aim. It helped me function. But *you* are what kept me going all these years," she said. "And you *still* keep me going. You're *amazing*! You are such a brilliant, dedicated, disciplined and hardworking girl. Such a *good* girl."

She stroked my hair. I felt like purring.

"So don't think I'm taking an antidepressant because I'm your mom and that's an issue for me. I'm on meds so I can be a *good* mother to you. You *deserve* that. And *more*."

"Are you sure you still need to take meds? I mean, aren't you better now? I'm grown up practically, your job is fine, you have a boyfriend—"

My headache was still pretty bad but my mind had let go of something it had been clutching at. Squeezing, pressing on way too hard. And I could feel my muscles relaxing themselves, the tension drifting away. Mom's gentle hands on my head were dependably repetitive, gently reassuring.

"I've gone on and off Prozac, and a whole host of other medications. Lots and lots of times over the years, honey. Right now I'm off. Things are stable so I'm off. For now."

I dozed a little, she kept talking. I was in and out, my headache lessening. At some point, she fell asleep too. She was really snoring. So loud I woke up, but only for a few seconds.

In the morning I felt great. Mom made us poached eggs on whole wheat English muffin halves and I ate two of them. She poured me a Mara & Padilla Butterfly Stoneware mug of Starbucks fresh-ground Colombian coffee, suggesting that a daily dose of caffeine might help with my headaches.

Who knew? I used Coffee-Mate to make a super white latté and drank the whole thing. It tasted okay. Not great, but not bad either.

So from there, we kind of detoured into a new and improved relationship. Redirected by the night of mother-daughter bonding and all that. But seriously, I tried not to be quite so sassy when she split for weekends in Boca. And she didn't hassle me so much about everything in my life. We let one another be. And that meant the days went a lot smoother with me and Moms.

So that's what was happening while me and H8er were out of touch. Like I told you, life was sort of good for a while.

Then, on a Friday night in the middle of May, H8er came back. As usual, the girl just showed up.

The HuffPo headline I liked best that day was *Baby Bump Watch*. The article was about the A-list celebs who were suspected of having babies on the way. I took my time studying all the candid photos of models and starlets looking kind of fat and not wearing any makeup. They seemed almost like normal girls.

I was reading about Maggie Gyllenhaal. She's married to Peter Sarsgaard. Doesn't it seem like their names have just too many a's? It's like they have like extra toes or something. This made me worry about their baby. What would it be like to have them as parents, with all those extra a's?

Something hit my bedroom window with a loud *plunk*. I almost had a heart attack. WTF?

Another pebble struck the window pane. Somebody was tossing rocks at my bedroom window, which faces the front lawn directly above the driveway. I freaked. *Fuck me!*

I kind of rolled off my bed and crawled over to the window to peek out. What if it was Bradley? I wasn't in the mood to deal with him. Plus, I was sporting a Victoria Beckham Avocado Facial Mask. From a recipe I got off the Internet. I looked like a slab of moldy cheese.

Another stone hit with a loud *clink*. I ducked.

"Hey, genius girl, come out and play."

H8er.

"I know you're in there, man. Hiding out, wasting away in Nerdvana." She got louder. "G'down here right now, *asshole!*"

She sounded high. Or drunk. Or both.

I stood up. *Fuck off!* I popped the lock to open the window and stared down at her. What a jerk-off! She was grinning up at me. Dirty. Her nose was bleeding. It looked like she had a new tattoo crawling up one side of her scrawny neck.

I said, "Shhhh! Shut up, will ya?"

"What died on your face?" she screamed.

"Shut the fuck up," I hissed. "I'll be right there."
"Like a boss," she laughed.
"Fuck me," I said under my breath. And meant it.

PART TWO
SUMMER, 2012

Thirteen: Lock, Stock, and a Lot More Shit

M Y MOM HITCHED a ride to my high school graduation ceremony with Bitsy's parents, and the three of them sat in the front row. Mom wore Ann Taylor tip to toe: white cotton sleeveless turtleneck (ribbed) with a striped Ponte Straight skirt in black and white, and Hallie Cork Platform shoes in blue lapis. She looked strangely youthful, so having her there wasn't as embarrassing as I'd thought it would be.

Bitsy (who wore this neat multicolored vintage wrap-dress by Giorgio di Sant' Angelo) gave a dynamite speech, all about world peace and the child soldiers and stuff like that. I've got to admit, I didn't listen too closely. Before I picked up Bitsy in the Land Rover, I'd popped one of Mom's Luvoxes, swallowed a couple of Prozacs, and smoked a mad joint H8er had tucked in my underwear drawer. So I was lazy and hazy. But I was happy for my friend, she's such a brilliant save-the-worlder. And after the graduation ceremony ended, she was high, too, on relief and adrenaline. We hugged one another and, on *three*, chucked our mortarboards into the cloudless sky. High school was frigging over, we were *out of there!*

Our parents took us out to dinner at The Wharf. Casual, elegant, expensive. I ordered crab cakes and lobster claw. The adults drank champagne. Our window overlooked the

Intracoastal. Yachts worth more than small eastern European countries rocked gently at their moorings.

Mom had warned me in advance that Professor Dimitri was going to join us for dinner, but to my surprise, I really didn't mind. In fact, I felt okay about it. Mainly because I wanted to see what Bitsy thought of him. ("Whoa, hottie," she said afterward. "And I like his ideas on creative intelligence. He's cool.") Without telling me, Mom had also invited Trixie to join us. I was majorly surprised. Really, it was a super nice thing for Mom to do. She's never approved of Trixie. And to acknowledge our trannie neighbor in front of Bitsy's parents and her newish boyfriend? It was a grand gesture, done entirely to please me. I was touched.

I'm not sure what the Beckmans thought of our half of the party for seven, but I had a blast that night. Everyone was in a totally fun mood and we all laughed a lot at stupid stuff. Bitsy's dad's a major preppie. He actually dressed in an Armani linen sport coat and white duck pants and Bermuda tan bucks! He's short, bald, roly-poly, and *he owns chunks of Tel Aviv*, as my mom likes to say. He's got a lot of international clients so he's not around that much but, when he is, he seems unobtrusive enough. Bitsy's mom is Japanese. She's petite, strict, beautiful. She had on a silver silk sheath straight out of an episode of Mad Men (from Talbot's; I asked her) and like five-inch platform pumps. Marcus had returned to the John Varvatos department and he was looking casually wrinkled, hip as ever. Trixie's bright auburn wig clashed perfectly with her russet silk dress, a Versace knockoff. At least, I think it was a knockoff! Under the tight scoop neck, her up and coming tits were gloriously full. I caught Professor Dimitri checking them out, and he saw me looking at him looking. He grinned and, sorry to say, I smiled coyly in return.

More than enough bonhomie to go around that night.

You believe me when I say I didn't want to hurt any of these people, right? I mean, not to go all emo, but they loved me, or at the very least they were pretty damn nice to me. Why would I want to hurt them?

But that night was the last of the little happiness bubble I'd floated in for those sweet weeks before summer dragged into town. The next chapter of my life loomed empty, unfriendly, with its dog days, heat haze, and violent thunderstorms. I turned some invisible page and a rainbow bubble popped and my life plummeted. Straight down into the deep shit.

First off, the job scene sucked ass. Ongoing recessionary woes meant few if any openings for teenagers like me. Especially in Florida in the summer, when the hotel and restaurant and mall fashion industries cling by their chawed-up fingernails, praying not to go under. Businesses make do with few employees until the brutal winter arrives up north to drive the customers down I-95 again. So, instead of an impossible-to-get low-wage job, I ended up signing up. For summer school classes at HSC.

Six of them.

Mom's idea. Not mine.

I'd wanted to spend the summer reading some of the great classic literature I'd missed out on in my lowest common denominator classes in high school. Professor Whitehead had sparked my interest. I felt lit crit undernourished, developmentally delayed intellectually. I couldn't quote Chaucer at the right moment, recite Shakespeare at the dinner table. I wanted to do things like that. I had also decided to get serious about my writing. Poetry, some creative nonfiction, one well-written story was my goal for the summer. One really good story, something I could be proud of.

Instead, Mom got influenced by Professor Dimitri, who somehow convinced her it would be in my best interest to get a whole semester of freshman classes out of the way by taking them over the summer. He said he'd use his influence to sign me up, because freshmen were not allowed to enroll until the fall. At HSC, summer classes were attended by the students who'd failed their coursework during the school year. The nittiest nitwits. The laziest shits, the tardiest tards.

I'd heard the dirt about summer classes, so I resisted the idea of attending them.

"No way," I told Mom when she announced her plan for my summer.

We were just finishing breakfast on the Friday after graduation. I'd had like five minutes to relax. Now this.

"I absolutely refuse. No. Not fine with me. I need a break from academics." I was adamant. Couldn't she see that? "Summer classes at that school will push me over the edge, Moms. I won't want to go back in the fall."

"Don't be *ridiculous*, Aim. This is HSC we're talking about."

Her no-nonsense voice was the giveaway. She'd already made up my mind for me.

"You can run *circles* around these kids. You got an A in your literature class, and every other course you took there. So you *know* you'll do well. You've said for a year how it's *easier* than those AP classes at Central. Less intense, less competitive. College *light*, right?"

All of which was true, but that wasn't the point. She was missing the point!

We were sitting side by side at the kitchen island drinking coffee and nibbling on the hideous, pastel-colored, thickly frosted doughnuts Trixie had dropped off at daybreak. "From a client. Please, you two skinnies, get these out of my sight. My ass is getting fatter just knowing they're in the house."

Mom was still in her robe and slippers. Her hair was down and flopped about in unruly tangles. She looked a little pale, maybe because she hadn't yet got her head on, as she called it. I was dressed in a pair of Forever 21 overall shorts with adjustable roller buckles and a large pocket on the bib. Under which I was wearing an urban wifebeater. Both from Out of the Closet.

Mom sighed. I sighed louder and tossed the stubby end of a pink frosted cruller on the Jasper Conran Blue Butterfly Wedgewood plate in front of me. I frowned, focused on my coffee. *I'm staying, enjoying my coffee*, I thought. A line from *The Big Lebowski*.

Why did I know movie lines better than the important words of great literature? Maybe because by that time I'd watched the Coen brothers' cult masterpiece at least nine times. Like whenever I was stuck at home for the weekend. With or without H8er.

My mother washed off a couple of dishes, poured more coffee, bustled around the kitchen. I could tell she'd made up our minds for us and that was fucking that. I sipped my overly sweet, overly creamy coffee. It tasted like a hot milkshake. I had a mild headache. The acid in my stomach roiled. I'd wanted my summer for myself. I'd made plans for myself, plans I was excited about. I had things I really wanted to accomplish.

Now this.

Mom came over and slid a sheet of paper across the island. She said, "Marc has some suggestions for you. Here's a list of the classes he says you can still get into at this late date. He says if you call him today, before five, he'll enroll you."

"*Jawohl, herr kommandant,*" I said.

My mother the Nazi officer. I rolled my eyes slowly so she could see that I was dissing her while, at the same time, bowing to her command. Like a big pussy.

"Your neck is perspiring, Heidi," she said. My gut flared. Was steam coming out my ears?

She poured the dregs of her coffee into the sink and went into her room to get dressed for work. She was meeting a client at noon in Vero, then driving down to Boca for the weekend. She'd know soon enough if I blew off Professor Dimitri. So I had no choice. No effing choice.

I picked up the paper and stared at the list. My heart sank to my gut, where it was immediately engulfed in roaring flames.

H8er answered the phone on the first ring. "Whaddup?"

"*You* know. It's Friday night, I'm hungry, I'm thirsty—"

"Pick me up at the bus station," she interrupted. "I'll score us a dub sack. Any decent wine in the fridge?"

"We still have a bottle from, you know, next door. It's in my closet. I'll pop it in the fridge right now." My head throbbed unpleasantly in anticipation. "But I don't have wheels. I'm stuck here until she comes home on Sunday."

Cradling the phone to my head, I pulled the bottle of

Barolo out of my underwear drawer and carried it downstairs. H8er was quiet, thinking. I could imagine the cogs in her deviant brain, clicking over, meshing into a plan of action.

"So," I said as I opened the fridge. "Any suggestions?"

"I could call that dickhead, Bradley. But we're like not interested, right?"

"Fucking A right," I agreed. "Let's not complicate things." No *way*.

"So what about Ms Smartypants, your valedictorian friend? Want to invite her along? Then make her drive us everywhere? Our own private designated nerd?"

I burst out laughing. Bitsy and H8er? Hilarious. No way that would work. They'd hate each other. Like instantly.

"I think not," I said. "She's way too straight. She'd never want to go along with anything *you* thought up."

"Right. Blame me, Heller. Like it's always *my* fault that you fuck guys you hardly know. Or drink stolen booze until you get so fucked up you fucking black out. It's old H8er that makes you do shit like that, right?"

She laughed, but what she said was annoying. In fact, it kind of pissed me off.

"Maybe you should do your own thing this weekend, H8er. I have stuff I want to accomplish around here anyway."

"Fuck that, Heller. SMD! You have all summer to nerd out."

No, I didn't. My freedom in Nerdvana was about to get cut off at the knees. But I didn't want to go into my sad tale of duh college woe. Not now.

I closed the refrigerator door and leaned against it, thinking. I really wasn't in the mood to party, but I *was* pissy and it *was* Friday night. Plus, I felt sorry for myself. In like another week, I'd have to buckle down again and start pleasing teachers, reading textbook bullshit I didn't care about, writing papers about stuff I didn't believe in. Except for maybe English Comp 100 (with Marcus) and English Lit 200 (Whitehead again). Those classes might be okay. But the rest of the summer courses Professor Dimitri had selected for me were the kind of dumbed down requirements for all freshmen that were sure to bore me. The kind of stupid time-wasting curricular shit that I could totally fucking do without.

I groaned silently. *Fuck me!* In no time at all I'd be back to the effing grind.

"I have an idea," H8er said.

"Okay, shoot," I said back, struggling with an emerging existential crisis. Sartre had nothing on me.

"Hellz yeah. Shoot? That's what I'm talking about. Shoot*ing.* Let's go out to Bumfuck, Nowhereville, and visit your grandfather. Let him show us how to use some of those firearms he has sitting around, collecting dust."

I laughed. She had to be joking.

"H8er," I said. "We don't even have a way of getting you *here.* How the ef are we gonna get all the way to Retiree Ranch? It's like miles west into the saw palmettos and gator mud."

"I'll take the bus to the stop on Ocean Boulevard near the 7-Eleven, then hitch to your place. I'm waiting for the bus right now. Surrounded by fucking bean-eaters, as usual. If I screamed *help me, help me,* nobody here would do a thing. None of 'em would even understand. Maybe I need to move to New England or North Dakota, where they don't have so many fucking tamales."

"Maybe you should keep your voice down," I said. "You shouldn't say stuff like that in public."

"Nobody can understand a word I say, Heller. That's my point. I'm like invisible, white girl pissing in the wind. Anyway, see you when I see you. Peace out."

For no rational reason, I watched *The Big Lebowski* again while waiting for H8er to arrive. I took a few hits from what was once an active roach and fell into a kind of dreamy reverie in which I told H8er off. I yelled at her, explaining in a mean way how "tamale" was not the accepted nomenclature for Hispanics. But she laughed at me and said, "The tamale is not the issue here, dude. It's the pederasts I'm talking about."

For a while I half-watched the film, then fell into a deep sleep.

When I woke up it was dark. H8er was in the kitchen, talking to somebody. I heard her laugh, then say, "Well, it sure was nice talking to you too, Dads."

I jumped off the couch and snatched up the remote to shut off the television, which was displaying the menu for *The Big Lebowski*. My head was full of bowling imagery.

"Good news. She is rizen," H8er said loudly after the film's annoying theme song stopped its repetitive blare.

Shaking my head to clear it, I stumbled into the kitchen. All the overhead lights were blazing. She was sitting at the counter and her long pale legs were swinging back and forth. She had on my Converse zebra-striped high-tops, unlaced, just the way I wore them. It kind of freaked me out. Sitting there all cool with my mom's fave wedding glass from Tiffany's. And the bottle of wine from my fridge. Trixie's wine.

She grinned and said, "It's all set, duder. Dads said he'd be happy to buy you a car. But he says he's limited by budgetary restraints to a pre-owned vehicle of some type. I suggested a van. Which is what we'll need. In order to carry all the supplies."

I was groggy, and she was going on and on. I had no clue what she was talking about. Like she was speaking Spanish or something.

"Dads?" I said. "Dads who?"

She ignored me, heading for the crystal display cabinet to fetch me a wine glass. I slumped on the bar stool. I had to quit stealing Mom's Luvox. It made me feel so damn slow. But since I knew we'd be drinking red wine tonight, I had taken a couple capsules. *Prophylactically*, as Dr. Digger would say.

Not that Luvox prevented migraines. Taking Mom's antidepressants just made me feel less stressed. About my life, about my headaches, my hangovers. About whatever. My life still sucked, it still hurt. But I just didn't care so much.

H8er bubbled on. "And before Dads, I had a super fucking nice chat with your grandfather. He's all excited about teaching Agnes how to shoot a shotgun. I told him we want to learn about all his guns. The old Army rifles, the revolvers, the semi-automatics. He sounded pretty fucking thrilled to have us coming to visit. He's lonely out there in west Bumfuck. You're such a shitty granddaughter. You need to visit the old man more often."

Snickering and acting all high and happy, she pranced over to the stools and poured wine in my glass. I stared numbly while she swirled the wine around the hand-blown crystal and pretended to sniff the bouquet. I didn't laugh at her antics. I guess I was in shock, or trying to figure out if she was bullshitting me.

"Of course, he wasn't sure who *you* were until I said *Aimee is the daughter of your daughter Marlene*. Then he said you were *a good shot* and to be sure to bring you along."

She grinned. Proud of herself. Or laughing at me, I wasn't sure which.

"Wait. Back up." My head was spinning. I gulped some wine. "Did you say you talked to my fucking *father*? While I was *sleeping*?" I shook my head. Was I still asleep? "I haven't talked to Dads in like two *years*, H8er. Did he call here? What the hell happened?"

"You're also a shitty daughter, Heller. Dads sounded ever so nice on the phone. Like he probably really fucking cares about you."

She was smiling at me, but her eyes were dark, impenetrable, menacing. I looked closely. The iris wasn't blue or purple or even gray anymore, but absent of color. Her eyes were a flat and unwavering black. They were like holes into something, into somewhere else. Which kind of creeped me out.

"Did *you* call *him*? Wait. Holy shit, H8er! Are you kidding me? Tell me you didn't use my address book, my cell phone, to call up my dad and my grandfather?"

My voice was shaking so I slugged some more wine. It burned my throat going down. I choked a little. Had she put something in it, a shot of Stoli Hot? No, she couldn't have. I'd been watching her. Unless she'd added something to the bottle of wine before I woke up? My eyes teared. I felt confused, dizzy. I pushed the glass aside and stood up.

My cell phone sat on the granite counter next to the sink. I picked it up, turned to glare at H8er.

"Heller, I'm your real true BFF," she said. Slowly, calmly, like I was a bratty child having a tantrum. "All the things I do for you are just that: *for you*. I'm working on your *life*. And it's time for Aimee 'Heidi' Heller to leave the wussy bullshit behind and strap on a set of balls. Do you fucking *get* me?"

"No," I said. "I fucking don't. I mean, what does my father—who has seen me like maybe ten times my whole life—have to do with *you*? And my demented grandfather, who hunts possums with his rusty old Swiss Army rifle from like 1945? I mean, what the fuck do they have to do with *you*?"

She poured more wine for herself and sipped it. After a minute of uncomfortable silence, I sat down again. My legs were tired. Like I'd run twelve miles, which I hadn't. My desire to run had faded once Coach Meyer was out of the picture. I hadn't gone for a single run since track had ended.

So much for keeping on with my training.

She nudged my wine glass toward me and I looked at her. She nodded, all solemn, like she knew what was best for me. I drank it down. It tasted like shit.

"Didn't you say your mother had like bottles of antidepressants and other prescription meds in her bathroom medicine cabinet?"

I couldn't recall telling H8er about this, but I guess I must have.

"So?" I said. "Another thing that doesn't have anything to do with you."

"Dude, you're being very undude," she said. "Let's go check out what she's got. We'll need some stuff for D-day."

"D-day?" I said. "Is it me or are you talking in some new code? What the fuck is D-day?"

"Okay, yeah, it's *code*. *Our* code, doofus. D is for Dude. Like Dude Day. And Dude Day is when we're gonna pull off the biggest girl-sponsored mayhem ever. Got that?"

I stared at H8er. Her eyes were so dark and flat they were kind of like black mirrors and I sort of bounced off them. Or fell into them, or something.

"Dude Day?" My giggle sounded wet, like I was drowning, going under. "Are you joking?" But I knew she wasn't, which scared me. My head did a rumba and my hands shook until I clasped them together. "Is this more H8er BS?"

"No shit, Heller. We are the DJs of our own life soundtrack, man. We're heroes, you and me. We're legends in our own minds, girl heroines for the college loan generation. Like Manson says, we wish we weren't us. Right? But we'll do what they won't do. Cuz we hate, therefore we are."

I understood her twist on the Manson lyrics. But wasn't the rest of the song something about slitting my teenage wrist?

H8er said, "You know what makes the greatest impression on the pussy world? The unmistakable sound of a pump-action shotgun in a crowded room. Especially in a classroom. Like at Dork U. Think about it. Us. Them. All quiet. And then, crunch, crunch."

She laughed. I said nothing. What I was thinking was, there's an unspoken message here.

The unspoken message was *leave me the fuck alone.*

H8er drank her boosted wine, then let out a manly burp. The fresh, raw tattoo on her neck was in a tiny, Asian-looking font. The words were in English, though. *Do Unto Others, But Worse.* Her pierced lip was red, scabby, infected. I wanted to sterilize her wine glass in boiling water.

She stood up. "Now, come with. I'm going on a fact finding mission to determine the extent and usefulness of Momsie's meds trove. We need to get fucking serious here, man. Time is of the essence. We have to make our plans, lock, stock and all that shit."

She turned and headed for the master bedroom, yelling over her shoulder, "Luvox for enhanced aggression! Zoloft for suicidal thoughts! Ambien for impulsive sex . . ."

She sounded like some warped pharmaceutical ad on Comedy Central.

What could I do? I got up and followed her in. I didn't want her messing up my mom's bathroom. I had enough shit to deal with without hearing it from Mom about that.

Fourteen: A World of Pain

I WAS LYING on my bed rereading *Ariel* and marveling at the linguistic beauty of Plath's anger when I heard the crunch of tires on shell and stone. My heart lurched and I dropped the book.

Since graduation I'd been having this like feeling of dread. Basically all the time. Every day I woke up full of a misty apprehension, like something major but not identified was wrong with me or my life. A tired blah feeling weighed me down, and a neurotic Woody Allen type of existential doom pressed on me, making it difficult to even get out of bed. The day went on like that sometimes, and lazing around was the best I could do.

Mom pulled into the driveway and shut off the car. My window was open a few inches so I felt like she'd just parked in my head. The day had been rainy and dark. Gloomy, wet, and fecund.

I inhaled deeply: wet cedar mulch, damp grass, and Trixie's magnolia blossoms. Yum. Car exhaust. Ick.

Mom got out of her SUV and rustled around in the back, retrieving her work stuff and, most likely, takeout from Paisley's. She grunted, muttered to herself, slammed car doors. She hadn't been in the best mood lately. But neither had I. We were both walking on eggshells, waiting for the other person to fly off into a homicidal rage.

I didn't want to ask Mom about Professor Dimitri. She

didn't want to ask me if I was okay with starting summer school. So we weren't talking much. Life with two women on the edge can feel downright dangerous.

Dangerous but necessary? Perhaps.

"Hi there," Mom called out in a fake cheery tone. Not to me, though. "Good, good," she lied. "How-bout you, Trixie?"

Trixie came over and the two of them stood in the drive-way, right under my window, talking in low voices. I had little interest until I heard what sounded like my name. Then I heard it again. Distinctly.

SMD! I had to know what they were saying about me.

I slid off the bed and crawled over to the window. I didn't dare peek over the sill because they could easily look up and catch me spying, so I crouched low. And aimed my ear toward the window screen.

No way I could hear everything they were saying, but I did catch one word that pumped up the dread. *Drinking.*

Oh-oh. I was in the shit now.

A little while later, Mom called me down for dinner. When I said I wasn't hungry, she got real pissy.

"Come down here. Right now," she commanded.

Heil Hitler, I thought. I tossed the Plath book on my bed and sat down at my laptop. I wrote a note to myself to finish the book.

If I didn't write notes to myself, who would?

While washing my hands in the bathroom sink, I stared at myself in the antique white French Inlay Mirror by Horchow. There were raccoonish circles under my eyes, and my new haircut made my face look stark, boyish. The row of tiny gold studs in my right eyebrow flashed light, but on the whole, I didn't look so good. Mom would probably start on that, too.

The kitchen smelled like garlic rolls and *maduros*. "I stopped at Caribbean Grills," Mom explained. "I didn't feel like cooking tonight."

Like this was news. I nodded, setting out the Wedgewood plates while she manned the microwave. A bottle of Malbec sat on the kitchen island so I got out one of her Riedel Bordeaux wine glasses and put it by her plate.

While I folded a couple of Irish linen napkins (in ecru), Mom sat down. She said in a fake casual voice, "Would you like a glass of wine, Aim?"

"No, thanks."

Ha. Not gonna fall for that silly ploy. If she wanted to accuse me of underage drinking, she'd have to be straight up about it. Then, of course, I would lie to her face.

She served me way too much *congris* and a half-breast of Cuban chicken with onion and mushroom sauce. I nibbled a hot plantain. My appetite was nonexistent. I craved marijuana. A cigarette. Ambien. Something to calm the ragged edges of my nerves. The anticipation of getting verbally attacked by Mom was making my hands shake. I decided to take the offensive.

"Moms—" I started.

At the exact same time, she said, "Look, Aimee—"

We glanced at one another and kind of laughed.

"You go first," she said. A black bean was lodged between her front teeth. It made her look like a homeless person. I didn't tell her this.

Instead, I said, "Is something going on with you and Professor Dimitri? I don't want to walk into my first day of classes on Monday and get the hairy eyeball from him."

Mom sighed and drank some of her wine. She looked tired.

Her hair was springing out of her hand-painted Spanish mantilla clip, tumbling down around her face. There were a lot of little wrinkles around her mouth and eyes, more than I'd ever noticed before. The overhead light was harsh. It was probably making me look crappy too.

"Marc and I are having *problems*, Aim. You're very perceptive."

Duh, I felt like saying. I could *perceive* Mom's relationship problems like I was reading about them in a favorite book. A story I knew by heart: instant infatuation, short-lived "love", a temporary high followed by the dark revelation (OMG, there was *someone else* in his life: wife, live-in lover, new flame, whatever? What a shock!), followed by massive heartbreak and months of wound-licking. Same old story, over and over again. Watching Mom go through one of her romances was like watching *The Big Lebowski*. I almost had her love life memorized. I certainly knew my lines.

"Is there someone else?" I asked.

Of course there was. The question was, did Mom know about her (or them) yet?

"No, nothing like that," she said. "He's just distant. Keeps me at a distance. It drives me *crazy*. I don't understand why anyone would want to spend so much time *alone*."

"I do," I said. "He's a writer. He spends all day with stupid HSC students. He needs time by himself so he can write. Don't take it personally." I didn't mean to defend the guy. I figured he was guilty of something. But in a way, I was defending myself. "I need to be alone a lot too," I added. "So I can get inside my own head. For writing purposes."

She looked at me skeptically. "Oh, for *writing* purposes. I see. I thought maybe when you were alone here, you liked to drink up my wine, steal my prescription antidepressants, sneak over to Trixie's and take some of her liquor. Things like that. But I see now I was *wrong*. You would *never* do something like that. You're too busy *writing*."

Her tone was mean but not, surprisingly, as angry as I'd expected. When I started to defend myself, she interrupted.

"Please, Aimee. Let me finish. I have something else to say."

I pushed the greasy *maduros* around my plate with a fork. Suddenly, she leaned over and snatched up the plate, startling me. Her eyes were big and round, bulging like a couple of fried eggs. *Oh, shit, here we go*, I thought.

"What is *wrong* with you, Aimee? You've *changed!* You're like a different person, an absolute stranger. You sulk around here all day in your crummy reclaimed clothes. You don't think I know where those outfits come from? I'm not as stupid as you think. I know a lot more than you'd like me to."

She waved a fork at me. A clump of black beans on the tines flew off.

"You don't eat right anymore, you sleep weird hours. I hear you up all night, wandering the house like some ghost. What is it you're doing all day, anyway? You're not working or running track, so it's no wonder you're not tired at night."

Her voice hardened. I shivered.

"And then Trixie comes over and says, in her polite, caring, shemale way, maybe you have *drinking* issues. You and one of your friends, maybe. Could I be any more embarrassed than today, with our neighbor insinuating you've stolen a bottle of wine from her? My god, Aimee, *what* is going on with you?"

I started to say *nothing*, but instead I said nothing. A bottle of wine? Trixie was such a cool person. She hadn't even fully squealed on me.

Mom continued her rant. Her hands waved around like she was Italian. She almost knocked over her wine glass like five times.

"And today at work your father calls. Tells me he's put a down payment on a 1999 Dodge Ram *van*. Your graduation gift. The one *you* asked him for. When were you going to tell me about talking to your dad? *Were* you going to tell me? And Aimee, really, a *van*? Have you lost your *mind*?"

I said, "Vans are handy, Mom. I can go to Home Depot and get trees and stuff for Trixie. Or pick up old furniture that people discard in front of their homes on 'big trash day'. Bring stuff home and repair it, paint it, sell it. Do stuff like that."

The words just spurted out. I didn't know where they came from. The truth was, I didn't want a van any more than she did.

Mom cocked her head and raised her plucky eyebrows. At least we weren't talking about the wine. I almost reached over and took a slug of hers. That would have spun her head around. I had to put my hand over my face to hide my smile.

"Are you fucking with me, Aimee? Because if you are, I really don't appreciate it."

I said nothing. She sighed.

"Look. Drinking my wine and fooling around with my pills is normal teenage stuff. If you and Bitsy snuck over to Trixie's and took some of her liquor, though, that's much more serious. I want you to repay Trixie whatever you owe her. Go talk to her. Find out what you can do to make it up to her."

I almost laughed at that. Bitsy, stealing? Fucking hilarious.

"And you'll be sorry when all the kids at school tease you about your piece of crap *van*. Really, Aimee. *Ridiculous*. You could have milked Uncle Moneybags for a nice e-class car like Bitsy has. Or a cute little Mini or something."

She shook her head, stood up to clear off her plate. It was amazing, she seemed more upset about my choice of low-class automobile than about the stealing. I stabbed a plantain and ate it in two quick bites.

Cold, but greasy and honey-sweet. I licked my lips, ate a couple more.

First day of summer classes I saw this: High School Teacher Taunts Students With Gun. A striking HuffPo headline, one I was enticed enough to click on. Turns out the guy was demonstrating something in a summer school class. It wasn't even his gun, he'd borrowed it from another teacher. And it had blanks in it, not bullets. Too bad because now he was facing twelve counts of felony, one for each of the students he'd threatened.

That article made me think. Waving a gun in a classroom could turn out way worse for you than you might guess.

But later, after spending a week in Professor Dimitri's composition class, I was wishing I had access to an AK-47. Yeah yeah yeah, we're all gonna die. Meantime, I wanted an assault rifle. Something big and hard and masculine and fatal. Because I'm not shitting you when I say my prof deserved to be shot. Right off the pedestal he thought he deserved to be up on.

First off, all the students were in love with him. He made that happen, he totally got off on it. So he was good-looking, mature, suave, hip? So what? So he made sure we all knew it. And he made us all acutely aware that he'd been published in like *Paris Review* and *The New Yorker*. Big whup lit mags. And that he was writing the next Great American Novel.

He told the class how he went to college at NYU with Jay McInerney. Like a hundred million years ago.

Did the dinosaurs chase you home from school, I wanted to ask him.

But you should see the way the kids in his class looked at him all googly-eyed. The same way Mom acted around him, all bristly and electric, all moony-faced and thrilled to have his attention. Now, in school every single weekday, I was surrounded by a room full of Marcus Dimitri fans. Assholes on parade. Watching the scene around me actually made my skin crawl.

To make the discomfort worse, he was like the biggest flirt on the planet. With the male students *and* the female ones. Like he had no discretion at all. He would look students right in the eye, saying their names, acknowledging them as *serious writers* with something *important* to say.

Please. Come on! He knew as well as I did that these kids were like so lame-assed. Most of them had zilch going on in their heads. What could they write about? MTV, dorm life, how to text and drive, the best way to make a beer bong?

Sitting in that class was the most torturous hour of my day. The other classes sucked, they were like television shows aimed at the brain dead. Only Professor Whitehead's class kept me from slipping into a late-afternoon coma. In fact, when he assigned *A Tale of Two Cities,* I almost had an orgasm, I was so excited. Dickens! I love Charles Dickens.

The other students groaned. *Oh no, we have to read a real book?* I'm sure online sales for the CliffsNotes version doubled, like overnight.

Then it happened. I dragged into English Literature 200 on the second Wednesday of classes, mildly hungover, a touch headachy, so I didn't notice right way. But when I collapsed into a seat in the front row and looked up, I almost screamed.

Professor Dimitri stood at the lectern in a pair of cargo pants and a khaki sports coat by (you guessed it) John Varvatos.

"Thank you for joining us today, Miss Heller," he joked.

Everyone laughed. I could feel the blood rush to my face.

"I was just explaining to your fellow students that Professor Whitehead is undergoing surgery. Right now, as we speak. Unexpected. So I've been elected to take over his classes for the remainder of the summer. Which will wreak havoc with the deadlines for my novel," he added with an exaggerated, totally self-conscious sigh. *Hint, hint. Ask me about my work of genius.*

Predictably, obediently, hands shot up. Professor Dimitri feigned surprise. He pointed to a kid in the back. "Yes, Diego?"

"What's your novel about?"

Ten free points for Diego. Ass kisser.

"So glad you asked," Professor Dimitri said. Everyone (except me) laughed. "I'm on the umpteenth draft of a literary novel, an epic family saga that crosses genre boundaries. Sort of a blend of suburban existentialism and erotic suspense."

"Sounds like a Tom Perrotta novel," someone said.

I turned around to see which of my classmates might have actually read a contemporary novel. A sunny, bleachy blonde with a gold hoop in one nostril and add-on breasts smugged from the third row.

"You flatter me, Veronica," Professor Dimitri said.

Of course she does, I thought. *Isn't that what you're here for?*

After an hour of us watching him preening himself, the

class ended. Everyone rushed up to the front of the room. They flocked around him, chattering inanely and jostling so they could be in position to talk to him while walking him to his next class.

I watched in horrified disgust. The whole scene sickened me. Some of the students rushed him after comp class too, but their love wasn't quite as dogged, not quite so deep and abiding. However, English Lit was a 200 level course and many of the students were English majors. Most had already worked with Professor Dimitri. They'd already begun to worship at the altar of Marcus. I sat among converts. These folks were diehards. I could barely stand it.

This is why, by early July, doing something as off the wall as driving out to Retiree Ranch with H8er and shooting semi-automatics at empty Coke Zero cans actually appealed to me. Because something was happening to me. Something dark and scary.

The darkness was there. It had been building up inside me for months, maybe for years, and the roiling in my gut had begun to boil and burble. Inside my primitive animal brain, deep in the ancient instinctual recesses, I was on fire. My head was actually hot to the touch. My nerves felt like they were shorting out, sparking, zinging like mad all up and down my body.

So maybe you can understand this. Once I was forced to face *two* intolerable summer school classes with my mother's stupid lover, a sort of straw that broke some poor animal's back, something inside me snapped. I let go of something. Like a foundation or a tether, a solid grip that had held me steady for years. *Snap!*

After that is when I really started to listen to H8er. I

actually began to seriously consider her ideas about D-day. Not a hundred percent seriously, but I did listen and think hard about what she was saying.

Because, like H8er explained, "We're girls for our time and place, Heller. This aggression against our dreams will not stand."

Which rang true. I mean, I really felt like I couldn't take it anymore. And why should I? I was tired of being toyed with, pushed around, told who to be and what to think. Why did everything I liked get tossed aside? D-day represented some kind of response to the world's aggression against me. Against us. Against girls in general. Against all those people who don't have much of a say in their lives.

Not a sane response, but certainly something to think about.

I imagined the HuffPo headline: *Girls Gone Wild on Florida Campus.* Or something like that.

Fifteen: Target Practice

I DROVE EVERYWHERE in my new-old Dodge Ram 3500 Maxi Van, and I loved it. Yeah, the engineering was from the Nixon era. And yeah, I looked like I was there to deliver flowers for your funeral. But I loved having my own wheels. Automatic, two door, rear antilock brakes, tinted windows, power steering, remote key entry, CD player with Infinity speakers, dual cup holders. What's not to like? I didn't care what the prep school snobs at HSC thought, I loved my white van.

But the first time me and H8er drove out to Retiree Ranch to visit Grampy, I let her take the wheel. Usually I drove, but that day I was out of it, overtired from another sleepless night, irritable and nervous. I had one of my headaches and my whole body quaked. I was actually kind of sick. Maybe because this was the first time anyone in my family had met Skitchen Sturter. I was worried about what my grandfather would think of her. Would she start swearing like a gang-banger and embarrass us both?

She was wearing my Diesel Lloyd leather jacket, even though it was like ninety degrees, and my Roberto Cavalli matte black jeans. She was driving and I was drinking a Bud Light Platinum (with six percent alcohol) and smoking chronic from this weird little pipe she'd traded for with some head down at the bus station. Every time I coughed, H8er laughed. Which was pissing me off.

"How do you think you're gonna learn to shoot like a man if you're half in the fucking bag?" she asked.

A rhetorical question. I wasn't going to learn to shoot like a man, *she* was.

"My B, Agnes," I said between ragged coughs. "But hey, you're the arms expert. Maybe I'll just sit on the porch and watch the sawgrass grow. You can go out possum hunting with the old man."

I chugged from the bright blue bottle. She frowned, hitting a pothole so hard I coughed again.

"You aren't taking this seriously enough, Heller. If we're gonna go down in history as the Columbine girls, if we're gonna make our mark for angry chicks everywhere, you gotta stop hiding behind your own pussy fears."

"Yeah, yeah, is there an unspoken message here, dude?"

My head still hurt but I didn't care quite as much. I took another hit, holding the hot, harsh smoke in my lungs as long as I could.

"There *is* an unspoken message here. *Don't fuck this up*," she said.

We were running lines from *The Big Lebowski*. I tried to laugh, but I couldn't. I held my breath for like a minute. My head lifted off my shoulders a little and I looked down at us, riding along in the Dodge Ram on the way to shoot off my grandfather's guns. I felt removed from us. And terribly unhappy.

What I know now that I didn't know then was that I was depressed. Seriously depressed.

What were my symptoms, you ask? Well, my symptoms were classic. Fucking classic! Number one: I was lethargic. I didn't even want to get out of bed in the morning because I didn't want to go to college. Or do anything at all. On weekends, sometimes I just didn't. Get out of bed, I mean. I just lay there thinking, or not thinking. Unless H8er showed up and bad mouthed me out of my numb stupor. Which worked. Otherwise, I might still be lying there. Which, in the long run, might have been best.

Number two: I had curtailed my activities. I wasn't running, volunteering, writing unless it was assigned, going anywhere unless I had to, eating much unless Mom made me, or even sleeping. Everything seemed too overwhelming, looming in the distance, out of reach, way beyond what I could handle.

Which links to number one. And to number three: I was withdrawn. I ignored my mother as much as possible, didn't talk in the classes I managed to show up for, sulked around campus like a morose shadow. *Leave me the fuck alone*, that's how I felt.

Thus, number four: I was irritable. And anxious. Because I was afraid of everything, especially my own inadequacies. I wasn't good enough, that was the overriding fear. I'd always sort of felt like this, only now this was all I felt.

H8er wasn't the least bit understanding. It really pissed her off, actually. Whenever I hid under the covers, unwilling to come downstairs for a glass of wine or a joyride in the van, she would scream at me, throw two shit fits, and guilt-trip me up and out into the world. She yelled at me while she did my homework for me, writing my papers and reading the textbooks out loud in a mean voice. While I lay on my back on my bed like a flesh dummy, washcloth over my red-rimmed eyes.

Because she was up my ass all the time, I kind of hated her. She knew it, too, but she didn't give a shit. She was all about D-day and making me join her for the big event. "Shut the fuck up," she'd tell me whenever I tried to kick her out of my room, the house, my van. "You're fucking this up and I'm not gonna let you."

On the way out to meet my grandfather, she drove past the citrus groves in silence. We left the trim edges of the suburbs behind, entering the no man's land of the Everglades. Graceful swallowtail kites soared overhead, and I spotted a red-shouldered hawk sitting on the top fronds of a cabbage palm, another one perched on a barren limb. When I pointed out a fat gator sunbathing on the embankment of the canal that ran parallel to the road, H8er ignored me. She kept her eyes on the dust and grasses ahead.

The July humidity hung like a hot, wet blanket over everything. It made me thirsty, even though I had just finished my beer. I turned on the radio, fiddling with the search buttons until I landed on NPR.

H8er reached over and flicked it off.

"We gotta talk," she said. "There's something I'm gonna need you to do."

I sighed. I knew what she wanted to discuss. By this time, H8er was all over the D-day plan. She talked incessantly about weapons we could use, places we might want to attack, dates that would have meaning, and specific ways we could draw the most media attention. None of her random vigilante shit interested me all that much. I tuned out a lot while she was yakking about it because, even though I thought her ideas were like mindblowingly intense, to me it was all a big farce.

Sure, I was angry. I was mad that my life was one long, dull chore. I was going to turn eighteen in like six weeks, and

I couldn't fathom how that meant I was still *young*. With so many years of drudgery ahead of me! It was all too much to cope with. I mean, at that point I didn't want to have to keep going on the way I was. Life was just chock full of ways to fuck up, so what was the point of trying so hard not to? I knew it was inevitable that I would only fuck up my life even more than I already had. It was unavoidable. Why drag out the world of pain I was in? Why not admit defeat now, and save everyone the burden of watching me self-destruct?

But marching into a crowded place and spraying other people with bullets didn't seem like the best solution to my woes. Plus, I doubted we'd ever be able to pull it off. Walk around campus with loaded weaponry? Enter a classroom and shoot innocent students? The whole idea was, in actual fact, ludicrous.

H8er hated it when I tried to tell her stuff like this. She didn't want to hear it. She was all about making a statement to the culture at large. Inspiring millions of girls facing social oppression all over the globe, young women she thought should take the opportunity to admit they were really angry. Because there were so many girls out there who deserved to be angry. About their unempowered lives, their lack of voice. About so many centuries of sexual repression, gender inequality. About how badly men were fucking everything up, and still bossing the rest of us around. Like why should we listen to *them?* Girls could change the world if they got pissed instead of feeling sad, H8er said. What if all the women in the world replaced their powerlessness, their internalized feelings of weakness and less than, with an aggressive stand for equality, justice, and the opportunity to be heard?

I myself had heard it all like a zillion times already.

"SMD, Heller! We're *more* than that, aren't we? We're not pussies, we're *pussy power!* The walking, talking, fucking symbol of girl power," she'd say to my stiff back whenever I lay on my side, unmoving, facing my bedroom wall. "So let's go out there and do it! You and me, Heller. Girls like us can get the rest of the goddam girl world all fired up!"

She had a point, yes. Today's women needed to stop letting everyone walk all over them. We needed to stop turning our pain on ourselves and start fighting back. The new feminism would involve taking up arms and using them against the oppressors. I knew that.

Still, all I wanted to do was close my exhausted eyes and get a decent four, five, OMG maybe *six* hours of deep, dreamless, sanity-restoring sleep. H8er's rants were interesting, mildly inspiring, even enticing, but only for a short while. Almost anyone could get off on the adrenaline rush of violent revenge fantasies. But I was too much of a realist to take her all that seriously.

So, by the dog days of summer, my own personal invest-ment in D-day was minimal at best. I wasn't sure H8er had accepted that fact. And I was too much of a pussy to tell her straight up that I was out. So, whenever she forced the issue, I went along for the ride. But I was only half there, if you know what I mean.

"What I need you to do, Heller," she said as we cruised along the access road toward my grandfather's bungalow, "is keep him out of the house for a good long stretch. I need to get in that gun closet. I'll need time alone without having to worry he'll come wandering in and fucking catch me with my hands in the cookie jar. I wouldn't want to have to hurt him."

"Oh, come on," I jeered. "What would you do if he walked in on you? Shoot him? A ninety-two-year-old with Alzheimer's?"

I scoffed, but her words bugged me. Who did she think she was, Clint Eastwood? Tony Soprano? Walter White?

"I wouldn't kill him, if that's what you mean," she said in this weird monotone she'd taken to using lately.

I couldn't see her eyes to tell whether she was fucking with me or not. She had on these black Balenciaga wraparound shades that looked suspiciously like a pair my mom used to wear.

"Unless you *want* me to kill him," she added.

"Cut the shit, H8er. Look: I'll be pathetic at target practice. So, if you want, you can sneak in the house and do your thing while I take an extended lesson from Grampy."

I wasn't in the mood to shoot at anything, but I wasn't lying to H8er either. It had been years since I'd practiced shooting targets with my grandfather. Plus, I was kind of stoned. I wouldn't be able to hit the widest side of a barn. Could I even lift one of Grampy's heavy-looking shotguns and hold it steady? I doubted that too.

Who cared anyway? What I needed was a nap.

I wasn't in the best shape, obviously. My ego had done a big nosedive, and my dreams had followed.

June had proven to be the beginning of the end for me at HSC. The long, dull, busywork days of summer school were even more painful when accompanied by an uneasy fear about the upcoming fall semester. How would I be able to get through the tedium? Mostly I felt flattened out. Invisible. The vague feeling of dread increased until it was on the verge of becoming an existential panic. Sometimes I felt like that famous painting by Munch, "The Scream."

Then, in like the middle of the month, my dad called my mom and told her the car was ready. Without asking me, Mom set up a meeting. So I could pick up my new-old van from Uncle Moneybags.

I was not in any shape to deal with Dads. He hadn't laid eyes on me in years, he rarely called me, he was like the tooth fairy. Good to have on your side, but not someone you wanted to deal with face to face. *Just put the dollars under the pillow and go, fairy.*

Plus, I felt like shit on a stick.

"Not fine with me. I can't do it, Mom," I'd said.

We were sitting on the back patio in the early evening dusk. She'd been crying, I could tell by the mascara smudges on her cheeks. Marcus trouble, no doubt. I didn't ask. We were watching the fat yellow moon rise up from behind our back neighbor's perfectly manicured ficus hedge. Next door, Trixie's television was blasting the evening news.

"Can't you go instead?" I begged.

Mom sighed. She was sipping a cup of herbal tea that smelled rich, darkly green. Earthy. If I hadn't been feeling like a wet noodle I would have gone inside and made myself a cup. But I couldn't lift my head from the gentle curves of the teak Aitali Chaise Longue.

"Hon, can't you just make time in your schedule to have lunch with him? I *know* he's an A-plus asshole, but he *is* your biological *father*."

"So? He's like a virtual stranger. Worse. Like an avatar. Avatar Dads. God, I'd rather endure lunch with Professor Dimitri. And I loathe *him*."

165

It slipped out. I was tired. Or maybe feeling mean.

"Whaaaaat?" She leaned sideways in her deck chair to study my face. "I thought you *liked* Marc. Isn't he a good teacher?"

I didn't want to tell her how much it sickened me to see him flirting with the kids at school. I mean, it wasn't really any of my business, but like everyone at HSC knew he was married. He had two young children too, and another one on the way. All his groupies talked about Mrs Dimitri. A lot of them had been to their house for parties. Supposedly, she was stuck up but beautiful. And intelligent, posh. From some rich British line. The salacious curiosity of his ambivalent marital status and flagrant campus affairs was the focus of much heated discussion among the members of the Professor Dimitri Fan Club.

That kind of crap didn't capture my interest. He was just a hound dog. The type of guy who always has several bitches on the leash at the same time.

Of course, I hadn't said a word to Mom about any of the dirty stuff I'd heard about him. But I'd been tempted. What was the right thing to do? Tell her and watch the hurt hit her like a speeding Greyhound? Or not tell her and wait for the hurt to catch up, then smash up her world?

"He's okay. It's just . . . I don't think he likes my writing," I told Mom. Which was true. In class he kind of made fun of one of my poems once, reading my work aloud as an example of what *not* to do when you want to capture the essence of something. "I think as a writing professor he sort of sucks."

I stopped there. I couldn't break her heart. I'd leave that to him. I mean, I was still mad at her for making me go to summer school, but she was so vulnerable when it came to men. Innocent, really. I felt like I needed to sort of protect her from him. He'd finish her off soon enough.

"Why, Aim?"

"He has his favorites and that's really lame. He's biased. He doesn't encourage risk. He wants us all to play it safe. He talks about himself too much. It's boring. I dunno, he just sucks."

Mom looked shocked.

"Maybe it's because he's a really great writer," I added. Mostly to make her feel better. I doubted he could write anything sincere and moving, something that captured our complicated humanity. He was most likely just another egotistical asshole.

"Well, this is interesting," Mom said in a harsh voice. "Because Marcus has done nothing but *praise* your writing. He tells me all the time you have real *talent*. He asked if I thought you might be willing to work for him in the fall. Help him edit the lit journal. Maybe work as a reader, eventually help him with his own work."

My jaw must have dropped because my mother laughed. Not a happy laugh, though. More like a here-we-go-again laugh.

"No way. He's messing with you, Mom."

"Interesting view. I'm afraid I'm beginning to see a *pattern* here, Aimee."

A pattern of her picking the worst men out of a lineup and then fucking them until they stabbed her in the heart? Was she looking for Mr Goodbar, or what?

But I didn't say any of this. I stared at the moon. Weird how it got bigger and bigger at first, like it was going to come down here and squish us, a big wheel of stinky cheese. But then, real suddenly, it got smaller and smaller, rising up and floating away in the blue-black sky.

"If you want the van, you'll have to do your own dirty work, Aimee. Go meet your dad. I'll drop you off. He wants to see you this Saturday. At Applebee's. The one at the mall."

"No way," I said. "Someone from school might see me. And their menu is ghastly. I'd rather eat at McDonalds."

"Call him yourself if you want to change the plan. Otherwise, finish your studies by twelve-thirty and be ready when I get here. I have a showing in Stuart, but I'll be back in time to drive you. And wear something *decent*. No Out of the Closet crappage, please."

The lunch itself wasn't so bad. I mean, Dads was his usual self. Pleasant, jovial. Smug, emotionally distant. I was like this wind-up toy he played with once a decade or so. He sat there in the pseudo-leather booth, smiling, drinking a light beer, watching me. Probably feeling all rosy inside about his generosity. Helping out his little bastard child, giving her handouts so she could make her pathetic way in the world.

He had on a salmon-colored Ralph Lauren Polo shirt, all neatly ironed and tucked into his Dolce & Gabbana Prince of Wales checked trousers with a DSquared leather belt. And a pair of goofy looking G & B Leather Mesh loafers. I had on my leather jacket because I'd been strangely cold lately. Applebee's kept the AC low, so I didn't take my coat off the whole time. Under it, I wore a dirty wifebeater. A pair of ripped jeans. Levis. Used stuff. Mom had been livid when she picked me up to drive me to the restaurant, but she'd let it go. Maybe she was too tired to fight about it. Maybe she secretly got a kick out of me looking like a hoodlum in front of my father.

I picked at a Waldorf salad and made rapid-fire small talk.

He joked around, tried to seem like he was cool. It wasn't as horrible as it might have been. But he didn't say much worth remembering.

At the end of like forty-five minutes, he tossed his black AmEx card on the fake leather billfold with our check in it. Then he handed me a set of keys. Car keys.

"If you get a single speeding ticket, I'll want these back," he said. All stern and everything. Like he even had any kind of say in my life.

I nodded solemnly. "Right, Dads," I said. "Gotcha."

We went out to the lot and there it was. I drove home, sitting way up high in the driver's seat.

Like I said, I loved my van right off. It was just so cool to be able to drive wherever I wanted whenever I felt like it. I never went much over fifty-five, because it was an old car and it kind of shook if you tried to push the pedal to the metal. But really, I was choosing not to get a speeding ticket. I didn't give a shit what my father wanted me to do or not do. I didn't. How could I?

Except for my wheels, however, my life wasn't feeling very good. Not sure why, but my dark mood darkened even more after the lunch with Dads. If I was like a clinical psychologist, maybe I could figure out why, after less than an hour with the old man, I wanted to curl up and disappear. But I'm not gonna try to figure that shit out. I really don't know myself very well at all.

Obviously.

Since the shocks weren't all that terrific, we jounced along pretty hard on the dirt road to Grampy's place. I started to feel pukey and my headache got a lot worse. When we pulled up in front, my grandfather was on the porch waiting for us. In one of his Tennessee rockers, a shotgun across his lap.

"OMG," H8er said. "If it ain't John Wayne Gacy."

"Shut up. You can call him Mr Heller."

"Kiss my ass, I ain't calling him *mister* anything. He's an old friend of Agnes's, remember?"

She laughed but her mouth wasn't smiling.

We got out of the car and walked up. The sun scraped at my skin until I felt clawed apart. The July heat is unbearable in Florida, but out in the Everglades it's like an evil punishment. Hell, or something like it.

But Grampy didn't have a drop of sweat on him. His leg was bleeding, but otherwise he looked pretty chipper. He was chomping on something. Chewing tobacco, I guess.

"Hey, Grampy," I said, leaning down to kiss his head. His bald spot was warm on my lips.

"Hi Agnes," he said, ignoring me completely. "You here for target practice?"

H8er grinned and said, "Yes, sir."

"You're skinnier than I remember," he said thoughtfully. "But I always liked those sexy little canines of yours."

He howled. He sounded like a sickly wolf.

I looked at H8er, shrugged. *Not all there.*

She nodded slightly. *Whatever the fuck.*

He stood up and led the way off the porch. "You might want to leave your jacket behind, Agnes. It gets awful damn hot out there in the brush."

H8er stripped off my jacket and tossed it over the railing. Then we followed my grandfather down the driveway, heading south into the high grasses along a narrow dirt path. Clumps of saw palmetto lunged at us, tearing at our clothes.

"What hell is this?" H8er asked me. "Man-eating jungle rot?"

I shrugged. I was too tired to think up a clever response.

I had a hard time keeping up. Me, the track runner, and I could barely see my old grandfather and my scrawny friend up ahead. The sun was directly over us and it kept trying to sear my skin off. Sweat dripped from my forehead into my eyes. The salt stung and so did like a million mosquitoes. I couldn't believe my grandfather spent all his free time torturing himself like this.

I caught up with them near a clump of tall cabbage palms. Messy fronds formed a canopy overhead that blocked the sun a bit, and there was the tiniest of breezes. It was quiet except for our heavy breathing, the annoying hum of mosquitoes, and an occasional tat-a-tat from a nearby woodpecker.

Grampy pointed to a single royal palm, a tree that stood ten feet taller than the rest of the wild growth surrounding it.

"That's the target, Agnes," he told H8er. "I'll demonstrate how to use this shotgun, then you can try to hit the trunk."

He ignored me.

"Now, don't worry about the recoil. That's a lotta bunk. Felt recoil depends on grip. Size and shape. So a gal like you can handle a gun like this, no problem."

He handed H8er the shotgun and said, "Heavy, right? Hold it in your hands there, get used to the feel of it. I'm gonna go over safety rules and proper handling. Next time I'll show you how to clean. Gotta know these things. As important as having a good eye and a steady hand."

Grampy acted like I wasn't on deck, so I decided I might as well not be. I was so tired I could barely stand up. I wandered away, backtracking down the dirt path until I spotted the wide branches of a reddish brown Gumbo Limbo tree. I ducked under and sat down, leaning my back against the wide, smooth trunk. All the dark green leaves the tree had discarded made a nice little cushion under me.

Soon enough, I felt pretty relaxed. My head hurt less. I stretched out on my back, listening to the industrious wood-pecker hammering away.

H8er laughed now and again. Once I heard Grampy howl. Eerie. When the gun shots began, they sounded oddly tinny, subdued. Everything seemed very far away, not part of my life. I closed my eyes and took a little nap.

When I woke up, H8er was kicking me in the ribs.

"Ow. Cut the shit," I said.

"Some help you are," she scolded. "So much for keeping him busy while I get the guns." She scowled. "C'mon, now we have to make a new plan. Hurry up, he's way ahead of us."

I rolled out from under the tree and staggered to my feet. Then I had to run to catch up with H8er. By the time we broke out of the underbrush onto the driveway, sweat was pouring down my face, between my breasts, under my arms. My crotch was soaked. And Grampy was nowhere in sight.

"Shit. He's gone inside. Fuck," H8er said. "You fucked it up, dude."

I couldn't protest. She was right, I hadn't done what we'd planned. But I didn't really care. It felt so good to fall asleep like that. So comfortable, so peaceful. H8er was the one who was all sexed up to get hold of my grandfather's arsenal. I wasn't into it. Not really.

But I didn't tell her that.

"You go inside and get him the fuck out here. Tell him you

need to talk to him on the porch. Once he's in the rocker, yak it up. You got to keep him talking. Can you at least fucking do *that* right, Heller?"

I shrugged. "He likes you, Agnes. Maybe you should talk to him out here while I sneak inside and get the guns."

She laughed in a mean way. "Like I can trust you to get what we need."

We reached the porch and stood facing one another. She gave me a cold stare. There wasn't a drop of sweat on her. Her wraparound shades, her monotone voice, the stiff tightness in her bony shoulders revealed nothing to indicate she cared about me. There was no warmth, no intimacy, no feeling of sisterhood. Why exactly was I spending so much time with this cool fish? I had no clue.

"You better be with me a hundred percent on this, Heller," she said in a low voice just slightly above a whisper. "Or I'll blow your fucking head off myself."

I was pretty sure she didn't mean it, but a chill ran up and down my back anyway. What did I really know about H8er, other than the bits and pieces she'd revealed over the course of our time together? Where was she from, who were her people, had she ever been violent before? I didn't know. She was a fucked-up chick, of course, I knew that. But so was I. Only I didn't think, at the time anyway, that I was nearly as pathological as H8er seemed to be.

Still, she was the only friend I had left. Bitsy had grown distant again, withdrawing from our friendship in advance of her upcoming departure for Ithaca. Trixie was very kind when I stopped by to apologize for taking her liquor, but our relationship wasn't the same. She was totally chill about the whole teenage vandalism thing, but she took the cash I offered her. My graduation money from Mom. And after that, I hadn't seen her around. I'm sure Trixie didn't trust me anymore. I couldn't blame her. I didn't trust myself.

Of course, I still had Mom. But Mom was Mom. Distracted, bossy, moody, and moony over her love affair. And still insistent in her plans for my future. Her agenda for my life. *Heil* Mom. She wasn't my friend. She wasn't supposed to be. Was she?

Grampy called to us through the screen door. "Hold this open, will you?"

H8er held the door so Grampy could squeeze by. He set a green plastic pitcher of lemonade on a small table next to his rocker and said, "Go inside and get us some cups, will you, Aimee? They're in the cabinet above the sink."

I looked at H8er and she shrugged. She leaned against the porch railing and ran a hand through her short hair. She still wasn't sweating. Not a drop of moisture on her broad white forehead, no stains on the wifebeater she'd stolen from my closet. She stared out at the infinite grassland in its waves of green, yellow, multiple shades of brown.

I went inside and stumbled around in the dark until my eyes adjusted enough to locate the kitchen cabinets. I grabbed three red plastic cups and brought them outside. H8er was still silent, staring at the horizon. But while I poured us some of what was sure to be lousy lemonade, she gave me a quick nod and slipped inside the house.

"Well, Grampy, what do you think of Agnes's marksmanship?"

He coughed. It sounded thick, phlegmy, disgusting. His shins were both bloodied, but not enough to warrant first aid. My right arm was slashed up a little and one of my fingers had a blister on it. But I wasn't about to go looking for Band-Aids. Not now.

"You still in summer school, young lady?" he asked once his hacking had subsided. His narrow, sunken eyes studied me carefully, as if he'd just noticed me sitting next to him and needed to make sure I was real.

"Yes, but I hate it."

"Of course you do. I don't know what's wrong with that mother of yours. Just because she got herself knocked up soon after high school doesn't mean you're stupid enough to ruin your life too." He shook his narrow, spotted, caramel-colored head. "Your grandmother used to drive me nuts, pestering me to do something about Marlene. But what could I do? She was a wild one, that girl. She had urges, she couldn't help that. I was kind of like that myself when I was young." He stopped talking and let out a long, slow belch. "But it's different for a boy. You can go out and sow your wild oats and not wreck your whole life. You girls, though, you can't get away with that kind of behavior."

I nodded. Keep him talking, H8er had said.

"What was Mom like when she was my age?"

"How old are you now, child? Fifteen?"

"No, I'm seventeen. Eighteen next month, Grampy."

"Oh my," he said. "I didn't realize." He gave me a hard stare. "You look younger. Especially with your hair all chopped off like that. What'd you go and do that for?"

I didn't say anything and he clucked in disgust. "Finding yourself, are you? Well, let me give you a little piece of ancient wisdom. Don't look too far from your arsehole. Most of what you need to know is already there."

He laughed at his own joke. I grinned, just to make him

happy. I had no idea what he meant. I was thirsty and hot. The lemonade tasted absolutely wretched. No way I could drink it. My head was starting to throb. And what the fuck was taking H8er so long? What was she doing in there?

Grampy burped again, then let out a squeaker fart. He acted like nothing happened so I did too. He rocked in his chair for a while and I tried to match his rhythm. He had it down. It wasn't easy to keep up.

"Don't let Marlene's neurotic bullshit influence you, Agnes," he said suddenly. "Make your own choices and pick your own pathways. That's the best advice an old man like me can give you. It's *your* life, so do with it what you will. What's yours ain't hers. Remember that."

I nodded. He'd called me Agnes. Did he call *everyone* Agnes? Who the fuck *was* Agnes anyway?

I startled when H8er called out to me from the van.

"Let's go, Heller. Time's a wastin'." She beeped the horn a couple times and yelled, "This train's leavin' the station."

I held up one finger and said to my grandfather, "Can I use your bathroom, Grampy?"

"Of course, child. My shitter is your shitter."

He laughed, so I patted him on the shoulder and went into the house. I wanted to see what, if anything, H8er had taken from the gun closet.

The door was unlocked, so I pulled it open. The shelves my grandfather had built were mostly empty. Except for a rifle that looked as old as Grampy, a pistol with a bumpy wooden handle, and a hand grenade. Plus an old green Army jacket, and several pair of black rubber boots.

I slung the jacket over my arm and picked up the grenade. It was knobby and cold. Like a miniature frozen pineapple

176

with an iron ring on top. I tucked it into the back pocket of my pants and hoped it didn't explode and blow my ass off. If it did, I wouldn't be able to find myself after all.

Out on the porch, I pulled on the Army jacket and modeled it, turning all the way around. It smelled like pine needles and tobacco. It was way too wide but kind of on the short side. It must have looked ridiculous on me. Grampy nodded, grinned. What remained of his teeth were small, brown, nubby. But his eyes were sparky, shrewd, and lively.

"Go ahead," he said. "Take it. I won't need it again until the winter comes. If it does. Wouldn't be surprised if we don't have any winter again this year."

H8er beeped the horn again. "I swear to god, I'm fucking leaving you here," she yelled.

My face got hot and I said to my grandfather, "Sorry about that. I guess we really have to get going. Agnes needs to get back."

He kept rocking, serene, but his eyes watched me carefully as I approached his chair.

"Oh, *Agnes* has to run off, does she?" he said. "Well, okay then, child. Give me a kiss and I'll let you go."

I hugged his frail shoulders. He was like a bird, a trussed chicken, but when he hugged me back his biceps felt ropy, wired for action.

"You come visit the old man again. Next time I'll show you how to shoot an automatic weapon. We'll have a ball."

I laughed. Then I picked up my leather jacket where H8er had left it, and hurried down the driveway to the van.

When I stood outside on the driver's side, H8er slid over to the passenger seat. "About fucking time," she said.

My back to the house, I took off the Army jacket and flung

it in the window. Then I tossed in the leather jacket. Slowly, carefully, I removed the grenade from my pocket and climbed into the car. I leaned across H8er to put the grenade in the glove compartment, then shut the door very gently.

"Why'd you take that shitty jacket and a stupid relic from like the Franco-Prussian War?" she asked in a pissy voice. "Take a good look at what I got."

She pointed behind us but I refused to give her the satisfaction of turning my head. Instead, I said, "How about some shut mouth for a change?" and started up the car.

We drove along in silence.

Finally, after like five minutes of hostile silence, I asked her, "How did you get out to the van like that? I didn't even see you leave the house—"

"Ever hear of a back door, man?" She cut me off. "Fucking A. You're so out of it I'm surprised you didn't forget all about me. Did you write yourself a note: *Don't forget H8er back there boosting guns.* Shit, you were so busy playing the perfect granddaughter with your smelly old ancestor. Phew. What a fucking stink on that one. He's like a rocking corpse."

I kept driving down the dirt road that led to the main road out of the Everglades, but what I felt like doing was slamming on the brakes. What if I stopped here, opened the passenger door, and kicked her the fuck out? What if I just left her here in the middle of nowhere and let her find her way back on her own? Or not. Preferably not.

She said, "I got us a fucking great stash of firearms, Heller. Un-fucking-believable. Now all we need is to practice our shooting. These citrus groves are perfect. Plenty of cover, nobody around. We'll drive out here every afternoon and shoot for like an hour. Then we can pick a date and plan the attack." She hooted. "Yeehaw! Time for some serious social hygiene. I can't wait to inflict my pain on all those bush league richies and posers."

I didn't say anything. I was thinking about the time I was playing around with my iPhone and I asked Siri, "Who's your daddy?"

Siri paused for a few seconds, then replied in that tech-noblah, instantly recognizable, computerized fake-real voice, "You are, baby."

For some reason, this made me think. I mean, really think.

Sixteen: English Comp 100 Summer Assignments by Aimee H. Heller

I'M SHOWING YOU these two homework assignments for one reason. I want you to read them because you're familiar with my writing. So you should be able to tell quite readily: It wasn't me. Aimee H. Heller did not write these two papers.

Okay, so they have my name on them. I know. But even though both assignments were done in my name, they aren't my work. H8er is the author of both the poem and the essay, both assignments for Professor Dimitri's comp class. Read them. You'll notice right off the difference in our voices, our writing styles.

Here's the straight-to-the-heart about the subject: I got in so much shit for H8er's writing, that's what finally did it. Pushed me over the edge. I swear, that's exactly how it went down for me.

Up until this point, wasn't my life kind of normal? Boring, even? I mean, except for cutting up with H8er, which was pretty average shit, not too high up on the delinquency scale. Like I was just your typical recent high school grad, hanging around waiting for some kind of life to happen to me. Right?

But the unbearable Florida summer dragged on and on. And summer school at HSC was driving me UTFW. I felt like just being there was hurting my IQ. Then, at home,

180

whenever Mom was around, her preemptory nostalgia about her soon-to-be-over love affair did a number on my head. Meanwhile, I had to sit in her lover's class and deal with his egotistical banality. Are you kidding me? Living in the middle of that conflicted shit was totally schizophrenogenic!

What you should know is, by early August I was in really horrible shape. My head hurt all the time and I never slept and I felt like roadkill. My eyes looked like a goat's butthole, ringed and wrinkled. My bones clinked against each other and my hips jutted out like a starved cow's. I was like a petting zoo. Maybe I smelled that bad, too, I wouldn't be surprised.

As Woody Allen once said, my life was like a vast desert of unspeakable doom. Or at least that's how it felt. My thirst was immense and I had zero energy. I literally dragged my body around like an overloaded pack-mule. A listless jackass.

In my condition, most of the time there was no way I could complete all my homework, especially the assignments for my comp class. I could not for the life of me think up a new, unique, or creative topic, or an interesting way to express myself. Sometimes days would pass and I would be unable to recall having a single coherent thought. I was like *so* out of it. My brain was washed. Acid washed.

So that's what you need to understand. Why H8er completed the two assignments I'm showing you. Instead of me.

At first I didn't want her to "help" me with the writing homework, but she insisted. You know how she is. So eventually I gave in. I mean, why not? I guess I thought it might be okay for her to do some of it. Because I wasn't keeping up. I was sinking under a growing mound of incomplete assignments, papers and reports, reading lists and take-home quizzes, a mounting pile of meaningless crap.

I was surprised when she volunteered to do the writing for me, but H8er said she had stuff inside her head that she wanted to get out. Thoughts and ideas. I never knew that about her, she'd never voiced a desire to write. I thought it was cool so I said okay. Go for it. Because I sure as hell couldn't muster up the requisite energy and enthusiasm.

So H8er wrote. When she was done, I would read over her work. Not bad. Most of the lines were pretty decent, not so different from what anybody in my class might come up with. We're talking an intro class for college freshmen here, nothing a motivated chimp couldn't handle. Usually I would go over whatever she wrote for me, proofreading, correcting her spelling, maybe making little corrections here and there. I was grateful for her efforts.

I lay on my unmade bed a lot of the time while she sat at my desk, her bony back hunched over my laptop. I could count her spine bones from like ten feet away.

In early August, right before the end of the summer semester, I must have totally blanked or something. I was hurting real bad by then, and on the verge of telling my mom we should make that appointment to see Dr. Digger. Somehow, maybe while I was in a Prozac and Stoli haze or something, I handed in two composition assignments H8er had done. This time without reading them over. I just gave them to Professor Dimitri.

What was I thinking?

I *wasn't* thinking. I totally wasn't. Aimee Heller was so out of it by that time, she really wasn't doing *any* thinking.

Go ahead and read the two papers. Then just imagine what I had to listen to after Professor Dimitri read H8er's work. OMG, he was merciless. He wasn't exactly nice in his critiques of my writing, but H8er's unabridged rantings? Fuck me. He took her ideas, her words, seriously. Like he had no sense of humor, and he went totally off on it.

What happened was, he nabbed me the second I snuck into class, late as usual. I headed for a seat in the back row and the class fell silent. Professor Dimitri had stopped talking—a rarity—so he could stare at me. His eyes were heavy lidded, cold. He looked old and mean. Like a giant lizard guarding it's young.

I was clueless. I had no idea he was pissed off about the work I'd handed in. In fact, what I thought to myself was, *Looks like Mom's dropped him. Good for her.*

I slumped into a desk chair and focused on unloading my backpack. The silence continued. Why punish the daughter for the sins of the mother? Besides, my mother never dumped a guy. So WTF? I didn't dare look up. My face felt like I'd dipped it in Mexican hot pepper soup.

When he finally spoke, Professor Dimitri enunciated carefully in this snotty, teacherish tone, "Meet me in my office directly after class, Ms Heller."

I nodded without looking up from my notebook full of doodles. This was a first for me. All summer I'd successfully avoided personal interaction with Professor Dimitri. We rarely spoke in class, and we ignored one another around campus. I'd liked it that way. He probably had too. Our lack of involvement allowed him to pretend to be an uninterested party while he led my mother on with empty promises about helping my budding career. Ha fucking ha.

SMD, Marcus.

After class I dry-swallowed two Advil Gel Caps while the Professor Dimitri Fan Club clustered around him, fawning and giggling. The group escorted him out of the classroom. Revolting. I followed them across the sweet smelling grass, maintaining a safe distance until we arrived at the four-story brick building that housed the English Department offices.

When I walked into his small, book-lined office, Professor Dimitri decreed to his hangers-on, "Okay, all of you, out." This really slutty-looking Hispanic girl who always wrote about incest in a pervy, icky sex way, started to pout. But Marcus gave her a thumbs out and, like the rest of them, she hurried off. He closed the door behind them.

Expecting the worst and not giving a shit, I collapsed in a cruddy metal folding chair at the far end of his cluttered desk. I stared out the small window behind him. The glare kind of blinded me. Perfect white clouds airbrushed on a baby blue sky. Campus lawns rolling away in plush green swathes.

A rhythmic pounding in my head reminded me of a Marilyn Manson song, but I couldn't recall the lyrics.

"Do you have an explanation for this?" His voice hung low, threatening to lunge.

An explanation for what, my lovesick mom's really poor life choices?

I shook my head, kept staring out the window. Down below, a group of male students stood around a cement bench, where a pretty coed with long blonde hair maintained court. Her occasional bursts of girlish laughter floated up to where we sat in a palpable, overheated silence.

Professor Dimitri rustled some papers on his desk. He sighed. Finally, tired of me already, he said, "Aimee, I could get into a lot of trouble for what you've written here. I could lose my job if I don't report this to the Dean. And to campus security."

What?

I looked over at his hands, toying with a small stack of papers on his desk. That's when I got what the meeting was about: My recent homework assignments.

H8er's writing.

"Aimee, what the *fuck* are you trying to do?" he spewed. "Is this about your mother and me? Because really, that's none of your business. You're here on campus as my student, not as the daughter of my, uh, friend."

Friend? That particular word choice must have been made specifically for the sake of the Fan Club. Who were probably loitering outside the office, ears to the door, listening to their idol lambaste me. Were the brown-nosers enjoying his tirade? Probably. Groupies seem to like it when their perceived competition gets crushed. One less potential writer in the world is, to the striving, an orgasmic relief.

Since I had yet to read what H8er had written, I was like totally unable to defend the work. So I shrugged and said, "A friend helped me write those two assignments. I'm sorry. It was wrong. I shouldn't have let that happen."

"Who? What friend? Someone in the class?"

"No, nobody you know. She isn't a student here."

This seemed to calm him. "Okay, then, that lets me off the hook. Which is a good thing. HSC does not approve of assignments that could lead to lawsuits. Even the faintest aroma of potential litigation makes those assholes in administration squirm."

Professor Dimitri had been squirming pretty hard too, but I didn't point that out to him.

He frowned. "But I'm not accepting this, um, *work.* I'm giving you two F's. Not incompletes, F's. And I'd like you to complete the two assignments yourself. Before the last day of class. And for god's sake, do not write on the same subjects your punk friend did."

He gave me this weird searching look. It was the most time he'd ever spent looking at me. I wondered what he was thinking. Did he think I resembled my mom?

With his thumb and index finger, he picked up H8er's papers, held them aloft. "Return these to your friend. And Aimee: Do yourself a favor and get yourself a new pal."

He held the papers out to me. By the edges. Like they were on fire. Or smelled of week-old shrimp, or clogged toilets.

Out in the parking lot, I sat in the van and read both papers. A poem. An essay. Both very H8er.

Professor Dimitri's comments in red ink, circled and un-derlined like ten times, were interesting. He'd labeled the poem "dangerous" and "seditious." The essay he'd called "scary nuts" and, among other things, "an example of the striking differ-ence between thoughtful writing and explosive diarrhea." If my head hadn't hurt so much at that moment, I might have laughed.

But the truth was, Professor Dimitri was right. H8er's writing *was* awful. It was truly bad. So bad that I actually learned something. Something important about myself. I re-alized with a gut-punch to my belly just how bad you can feel when you let somebody else do your talking for you.

Humiliated that my professor thought, even for a short while, that I had written the two papers, I shoved the assign-ments in the glove compartment. Then I drove home in a funk.

Later that day, when H8er and I were heading to the citrus

groves for target practice, I pulled out the papers and told her what Professor Dimitri had said. She laughed and punched the air above her head. Then she took both hands off the steering wheel to give me a double fist-bump.

"From now on, I'll let Smith & Wesson do *my* talking," she said. "Yeehaw! That crap college has no right to limit *my* fucking freedom of speech. Next week, Heller! We're taking those fuckers *down*. We'll make that fucking dickweed eat his fucking words."

I snorted. Right.

I still thought she was, as usual, just talking shit. Maybe because I wasn't getting it. Maybe because I was so tired all the time and my head was so fucked up. But really, I couldn't take her D-day plans seriously. I mean, come on: two dorky girls running around a college campus shooting people? I mean, *me and H8er* actually doing something like that? In my mind, Dude Day was nothing more than loser chick, Hollywood inspired, fucked up nerd girl fantasies.

Even then, even as late as early August, even on the way to target practice with H8er, I still thought that.

We'd been going out there almost every day after school. I'd actually become pretty good at firing rounds without falling over. I even blew a Bud Light Premium bottle off the stump of an old orange tree now and again. Especially if I was at close range. I mean like when I was right on top of the target.

H8er, on the other hand, could shoot the label off a bottle at twenty-five, thirty feet. She was a natural. The kick didn't bother her the way it bothered me. The noise of gunfire really got into my head. Made the ache that was almost always there absolutely ring my ears. Like I had a bell in my head that just wouldn't stop clanging.

A warning bell, maybe.

But H8er could stand there shooting one of Grampy's rifles or handguns without cringing, flailing or complaining. She loved it. Totally like a boss with a big fat .45 in her hand. And she knew it, man. She fucking reveled in her antihero cool.

I don't know for sure, but probably that's why H8er wrote the poem she gave me to hand in to my professor. And her "scary nuts" essay.

You take a look, see what you think.

GUN GENETICS BY AIMEE H. HELLER

Let's talk about x and y, xx and why
my guns are loaded, lock and stock,
and the girls in the front row cry
while the boys plot revenge.
I say nothing. Until now.

Let's talk how nothing's
faster than a speeding bullet
from my Smith & Wesson 460XVR
with the highest muzzle velocity
of any production revolver on earth,
or so it says
in the ads
and the X-treme Velocity
is what grabs me
cuz I'm gonna do it
fast. Get it over with.
End the world
of pain.

And nothing

provides better performance
than this,
my Smith & Wesson Crimson Trace
Lasergrips for ultimate target acquisition
or so it says in the ads
and me,
I acquire. The target,
my targets
at the speed of light
I can hold the point
of aim through thousands of rounds
of fire.
And this grabs me cuz

I'm gonna do this fast
so nobody
stops me and I
get it over with,
end the pain
and my guns help me
focus on the target,
my targets,
not the gun, as they say
in the ads.
Nothing but the guns

grab me and I grab me
a Bern Stg 51 Assault Rifle,
a W&F Bern Arsenal MP41/44

that fires 900 rounds a minute,
an Italian Beretta double-action
semi-automatic pistol
with 16-round double-stack magazine,
the U.S. version M9
(deluxe model with smooth walnut
hand grips and gold-plated hammer),
the M1911A1 Vietnam-era .45
so easy to find,
and a plastic camo-colored
Glock 21
with single-position-feed magazines,
global fave Heckler & Koch
MP5K short-barreled submachine gun
for close quarters;
the AK-47, that beauty
operates on a closed belt principle
not so practical
yet the most widely used
assault rifle in the world
does not jam
so you can fire, fire, fire
700 rounds a minute
and nothing stops

you and I will
grab us our guns,

not some pussy LadySmith
small frame revolver,
no compact

tuck in a purse pistol,
no sissy
stuff for us
cuz we're gonna do this right
like men
because, really,
when it comes
to living
in a world of pain
there's no difference, nothing
between
xx and xy, like

there's no why.

BLONDE ON BLONDE SPREES:
A WOMANIFESTO BY AIMEE H. HELLER

In case you been wondering, the inspiration for my new hair-style is the Gang of Blondes, ballzy chicks who are pulling off dozens of express kidnappings at high-end shopping malls in urban centers. These babes are all very blonde. They are also attractive, well-dressed, and successful. Like who I want to be when I grow up. Like who I want to be now!

The Gang of Blondes will target an attractive, well-dressed, wealthy blonde at a luxe shopping center, follow her out to her Mercedes or Jag or Porsche SUV, then hold her up at gunpoint. They keep her in her own car while one of the gang assumes the victim's identity and returns to the mall for an over-the-top shopping spree. Designer fashions, thousand-dollar shoes, gold jewelry, rings and bracelets studded with diamonds, rubies, sapphires, plus furs, leather jackets, some men's clothes, wool suits, and on to the electronics, laptops, smart phones, anything one can carry out in a bag, shopping on and on until the victim's credit limits are reached. The victim is then released unharmed, but the spree's over and it's too damn late to undo what's done.

There's no pussying around for these brave chicks. These blondes are all for one, one for all. Girl power in action. These women are beautiful, bold, smart, and unafraid. They don't hide in a puffy bedroom cutting their soft skin with an unfaithful man's razor blade, they don't stand before a harsh-lit mirror weeping over too-small breasts. They target desire and go for it, man! This is why my hair is white blonde now, in solidarity, and I feel myself grow blonder every day on the road to something more powerfully me.

Think about it: the next step on the path to gender equality for today's woman rests not in the bedroom or the boardroom, although there is still work to be done in both arenas. The next step up the ladder requires the undertaking—without male direction or control—of violent acts. Women fail to measure up to men in every area of violent behavior, except perhaps in cases of psychotic depression and other mental disorders in which the violence is most often inflicted on the self. Which doesn't count. What about blonde on blonde? And blonde on everyone else? This is what's missing from women's historic achievements in gender equality.

Violence begins at home, which is not a problem for many girls. There are plenty of chances to hone one's skills while engaged in the domestic aspects of life. However, girls lose ground because they so rarely bring the violence from home out into the world. They almost never bring it with them into the schools they attend. Yes, there are girl gangs, vicious cat fights, and certainly women do get into all sorts of scrapes. But why no female mass murderers? I don't mean the spoiled wives of dictators, women married to the mob, the supportive girlfriends of bank robbers and homicidal maniacs. Much more rare is the girl who stands her ground, firing before fired upon, going ballistic in a public space.

Personally, I see this particular gender gap as an opportunity and a challenge.

In 1979, a sixteen-year-old barricaded herself inside her family home and shot up the street for hours, targeting the local elementary school. She used a semi-automatic .22 rifle, a gift from her father. "I asked him for a radio and he bought me a gun," she said later; and then, as explanation, "I don't like Mondays; this livens up the day."

In 2008, a homeless college student in Louisiana bought a .357 revolver at a pawn shop and brought it to school, where she killed two classmates. Before shooting herself, she told her fellow students, "Don't worry, I'm not mad at you."

These are the only cases of mass shootings conducted by females in a U.S. school setting. The only ones! Both seem unimpressive when one considers the many incidences of school massacres perpetrated by boys.

Is this because girls don't become addicted to Doom and other violent video games? Girls may not play as much School Shooter: North American Tour 2012, or Super Columbine Massacre RPG!, or V-Tech Rampage. Maybe stepping into the imaginary shoes of school shooters allows the creative juices to flow in the direction of school violence. Such theories have been posited, but not well received. Similarly, is Marilyn Manson really to blame for teen violence because of lyrics that encourage listeners to carry out these kinds of acts? After all, most teens don't express themselves violently, no matter what games and songs they like.

The numbers of people shot, killed, wounded, psychologically scarred by random violence in American schools is incalculable. But it's impressive. Boys rule here. Girls, not so much. Why so little female representation with random acts of violence?

Come on, girls! This imbalance can be rectified. It's up to us. Nothing is stopping us. We can dye our hair white and take up arms. Because gun laws do not discriminate against the fairer sex. So we have only ourselves to blame if we continue pussying around, feeling powerless and afraid.

A couple days later I handed in a new poem, a dark one with a touch of wit, and a longish essay I could barely remember writing. Both had dripped out of me onto the keyboard. I was out of context again. I wondered, was that my real voice or not? I had no idea. Whatever I wanted to say was a locked room, a dream I could never recall once I woke up. It was strangely painful to write in this way. I felt like I'd taken a speeding bullet in the cranium. I sat through class like a shooting victim, holding my head in my hands.

The last weeks of school couldn't pass quickly enough.

On the Friday before finals, Professor Dimitri asked me to join him in the hall outside the classroom. My face burned as I scuffed up the aisle to the front of the room. The Fan Club glared so violently I could feel my skin sizzling.

We stepped outside and he closed the classroom door behind us. We stood facing one another. The hall smelled like lemon wax and cinnamon gum.

"What kind of shit are you trying to pull, Aimee? I'm going to pretend you didn't hand in that nonsense. I'm going to pretend you never handed in the assignments. Do you a favor."

He was dressed in one of his rumpled Green Day outfits. His hair shagged over his collar. I looked at him, shrugged. He shook his head like wonders never ceased.

"You want to be accepted into my program, you want to be an English major, you can't afford to do anything less than stellar work in this class. Serious writing, Aimee. Not wild-eyed diatribes. I'm giving you an incomplete this semester. Maybe you can take some time before school starts in the fall. Rewrite the assignments. Write for others' enjoyment, not just as a way to act out. In other words, get your shit together, young lady."

Which meant I had to take Comp 100 again in the fall. Along with two other summer classes I seemed to be failing.

He sighed heavily. "I had hoped you might work with us on the lit journal this year, Aimee," he said in a sad voice. Like he cared. His breath smelled faintly of overripe fruit. Maybe he was rotting intestinally. "Your work shows talent. You could create something worth reading. But you're inconsistent. You lack discipline. You have an axe to grind with me, obviously. I guess you're just immature."

Immature? SMD, dude!

My gut grilled what little was in there, and still, I managed to smile. I smiled right at him. Stood there smiling and smiling. Calm, cool, whatever. Immature? Try homicidal. Fuck his stupid clichés, his clichéd professor's life. Fuck his stupid lit journal. Fuck the goddam English department, his creepy Fan Club. Fuck him, the overgrown high school boy masquerading as a mature leader of youth. Fuck college, academia, all the deadening, mind-numbing lectures. Fuck summer classes, fuck higher education. Fuck it! FTW!

Still, I smiled, said nothing.

His fruity smell was overpowering, but I kept smiling. Like an idiot. Like a numb idiot.

He shook his head once more and said, "If you can hand in something written by a mature person, a poem and an essay that are worth my time, if you can get those to me by summer's end, Aimee, I will reconsider. You might still earn that A, and I'll allow you to sign up for Comp 200. Because I know what you are capable of, I'm cutting you yards of slack here. So take the rest of August to do a little growing up and try to produce some serious writing."

He glared at me before he turned and went back in the classroom.

I stood there for a minute or two with that half-assed grin on my face. I could hear one of my classmates' voices. He was reading a rhyming, absolutely craptastic poem. I couldn't bear it so I headed for the parking lot.

Enough school for the day.

Enough school forever.

H8er sprawled across the front seat of the van. I climbed into the back and unzipped the U.S. G.I. Military Surplus Army Navy USMC Duffle Bag in Olive Drab, the bag we'd ordered off eBay. I fondled our firearms, inhaling the greasy smell of gun oil.

"We need more ammo," I said.

"We sure do," H8er agreed.

She started up the car and drove out of the lot. I lifted up my tee-shirt and ran the butt of the 460XVR revolver up and down my hot belly. It felt cold, smooth, dangerously erotic. I put it to my mouth and stuck my tongue in the barrel. It tasted like the nozzle of a garden hose when you drink from it on a hot summer day. I French-kissed the gun while H8er watched me silently in the rearview mirror.

"Monday is the last day of classes before finals," I said, taking a break from making love to the handgun. "I don't like Mondays."

H8er laughed and said, "I know one way we can liven things up."

Seventeen: More Epic Fails

T HINGS GOT WORSE from there.

That weekend, the HuffPo headlines included these priceless gems: *Tara Reid Wore Dangerously Low Pants; Boy Sells Kidney To Buy iPad And iPhone; Students Tied Up, Coated In Hot Sauce;* and, my personal fave, *Girl Had Newborn Zipped in Purse.*

And I was the one in trouble? For writing a duh poem and a creepy essay? Or like for being friends with someone who wrote that kind of stupid stuff? I mean, kids my age were out there doing a whole lot worse. At least I wasn't coating fellow coeds in condiments, battering them up like Asian-fusion chicken wings. Or delivering a love child into my beige (with Light Tobacco leather trim) Gucci Heritage shoulder bag. Wearing baggies that showed off my ass crack. My coiled, ready to spring, youthful defiance. Crap like that.

Mom should have been proud of me for being so restrained. I mean, really, I wasn't some big swinging frat dick, a cock-knocker or a train-pulling twit. I wasn't tossing babies in dumpsters or selling myself in exchange for dollar meals. Right?

Not that I was surprised when I found out Professor Dimitri had squealed on me, because I wasn't. Not really. How could he *not* tell my mom what I was up to in his classroom? But the way my mother responded? Whoa. I mean, her reaction kind of shocked me. She had been so wonderfully self-absorbed lately, her nose up her own butt instead of mine for a change. So her anger caught me off guard.

H8er was upstairs in my room and I was heating up a Wolfgang Puck buffalo mozzarella, radicchio, and spicy chicken pizza, when Mom stormed in. Her hair clung to her face in sopping strings because sheets of hot rain had been coming down nonstop since early Saturday morning. Which explains why H8er and I were home instead of out doing some last minute target practice in the groves.

"Hand me the keys to your van."

Her voice sounded wet, clogged with tears or anger or maybe just summer rain. The navy blue mascara running down Mom's cheek bones made her look deep-sea haunted. Sharky, kind of scary. She held out a damp hand, wiggling the pale fishy fingers, demanding.

Jawohl. I reached into the front pocket of my secondhand Eddie Bauer Rain Pocket cargo shorts. Bubbling cheese from the pizza was emitting a sweet, nutty aroma.

"Is this really necessary?" I asked.

Rhetorical question. I didn't expect an answer. Not from the dripping *herr kommandant.*

Without any discussion, Mom snatched away the keys. Grabbed them right out of my hand. Then she grounded me. No going anywhere. For the rest of the summer. Her eyes were like coals in a barbecue pit. I swear I saw little red lights, sparks of unholy fire. My mother was possessed.

So I didn't argue or try to defend myself. No use trying to talk sense to her until she'd had an exorcist clear her body of whatever demon was residing in there.

She stormed out of the kitchen. The front door slammed, and I heard the Land Rover roar to life. She peeled out of the driveway. The whole neighborhood could hear her skid onto wet asphalt, then zoom off.

And, just like that, what little freedom I'd had was taken away. FTW!

Too late, I remembered the pizza and yanked open the stainless steel oven door. Charred remains of what might have been satisfying now laughed at me from inside our Bosch built-in double wall oven. Another taunt. Another reminder that I could never do things right. Even with the simplest things, my results were bad. I was never good enough, never measured up to expectations.

Might as well fuck it up all the way then. Why bother trying when, after years and years of self-sacrifice and butt-breaking work, you end up down in the dumps with the rest of the lifelong losers? Coated with condiments, or pregnant with some married guy's unwanted baby?

"Fuck it!" I yelled.

I grabbed the blackened pizza and held it up to my nose. It smelled like diesel exhaust. The crust was shiny as mica, hard as a rock. *Fuck you*, I thought, and took a huge bite.

Of course the pizza was piping hot. I screamed in pain. The roof of my mouth bubbled like a piece of toasting cheese. Bitter ash coated my lips. I coughed, then ran to the sink to spit out what I could. The regurgitated mess looked clotted, reddish. Was my mouth bleeding?

The doorbell rang. Had Mom reconsidered? Realizing she'd left me here with no way to buy food, get around town, or amuse myself all weekend? Had she turned around on I-95, retracing her steps to return my keys, chiding me instead with a familiar sermon on the care one needs to exert when self-expressing in a semi-public forum? Maybe a blessedly brief rehash of her famous how to kiss teacher's ass lecture?

I ran to the door and swung it open. Mom had her own key and the door was unlocked. Obviously, my initial optimism had been premature. So premature I could have zipped it in a purse.

Trixie stood on the flagstone patio holding the local section of the newspaper over her head. She was protecting from the heavy downpour the kind of honey blonde wig Dolly Parton might wear on stage. A drenched Burberry Alcester double-breasted trench coat in Hawthorne Red clung to and maximized her increasing buxomness. I imagined Trixie's surging bust popping off coat buttons, filling like thirsty helium balloons, lifting her out of her Jimmy Choo Leopard Print Pony Peep-Toe cork-wedge pumps (with five inch heels), and floating her off my front steps.

I wasn't in the mood for Trixie. Right at that moment, her surprise visit was not fine with me.

"Let me in, my makeup is running. Is Marlene home?"

I backed up so Trixie could step inside. She shook herself like a Golden Retriever after an unwanted bath.

"She just left," I said, closing the door on the pounding rain. "I'm surprised you didn't hear her. I'm sure she like woke all the late sleepers in the neighborhood."

"I thought all that tire screeching was coming from you," Trixie said, giving me the once over. "You're losing weight, aren't you." A statement, not a question. The local trannie offering me her woman-to-woman commentary. "And what's with the white hair? What is going on with you, Aimee?"

When she reached over to touch my bleached bangs, I flinched. She put her perfectly manicured hand down and fixed me with a hard stare.

"Okay, I see. I see," she said.

Pop psychology was flooding her brain. Adolescent hormone theory, prefrontal cortex development, all the bullshit she'd ever read online. I could actually picture her neurons firing excitedly as she flipped through archives of psychological tripe, figuring me out, shrinking me.

"Well, you're lucky your mom's not here. I was going to have another little chat with her about my mysteriously dwindling liquor supply."

Trixie waited for me to respond. She tapped her size thirteen foot impatiently. I'm surprised they make designer shoes in her size. Her feet are like the manliest thing about her. They're clown feet, no matter how many hundreds of dollars she pays to shod them.

Shod them? I sounded like I was talking about a farm animal.

She dug around in her coat pocket for something, then held it out for me to look at. A key. Another key that represented something I was losing, this time the freedom to access Trixie's private property. I stared at the little nickel tool until she closed her fingers around it. Her nails were French-style, her polish a girlish pearly pink. She returned the key to her coat pocket.

"I can't trust you anymore, Aimee. I'm sorry to say it, but it's true."

She clucked, an irritated hen.

Farm animals again. What was with me?

"Marlene can tend to my plants and my kitties when I'm out of town. Until you outgrow whatever this phase is you're going through."

What could I say? That I hadn't taken anything from her

house in months? But that my BFF probably had? My BFF, who was at that moment upstairs in my bedroom listening to everything we were saying?

I wanted to rat out H8er. I really did. That bitch was getting me in all sorts of shit. But all I did was nod and say, "Look, I'm not sure what you're talking about, but I'm sorry you feel the way you do. If there's anything I can do to change that—"

"You can be yourself, Aimee. Just be yourself. Like that tee-shirt you used to wear, the one that said, *Be yourself. Everyone else is taken.*"

Trixie managed to pat the top of my head. She toyed with what was left of my hair. I knew what she was thinking: it felt like straw from repetitive and self-inflicted (and ultra-cheap) bleach jobs. I stood there and let her pet me.

Now who was the farm animal?

She stopped in the doorway and said, "For god's sake, Aimee, be careful with that bottle of absinthe. It's an import, I got it from a friend. That stuff is extremely potent. Not safe. You can hallucinate, you drink too much of it. I really wish you'd just give it back to me, kiddo."

She stared at me until I shrugged. I had no clue. Absinthe? Isn't that the shit that drove Van Gogh mad?

She frowned. "Okay, then. Too bad for you. But for god's sake, please let me take you down to Klassy Kuts. Arthur is a magician with the scissors, the dye. He'll be able to make you well again. At least on top." She ran a hand through her fake hair. "Think about it, okay?"

When I smiled at her, the raw edges of my palate stung. Was blood sliding out between my teeth?

Trixie waggled her fingers over her head, waving goodbye

as she hurried down the front steps and off into the down-pour. She was always so kind to me and what had I done in return? I'd let H8er loose on her private residence. I'd ruined her trust. *Ruined* it.

This had to be a nadir, right? I mean, could my life possibly slide any lower down the cesspool shaft? Everyone was mad at me, nobody trusted me, I had no one on my side. Except H8er, and I was beginning to question whose side she was really on. Why did having her as a BFF feel like slipping a noose around my neck and wandering around a dark forest looking for just the right tree branch?

H8er loped down the stairs two at a time. When she shoved her hair back out of her eyes, I caught a glimpse of her newest tat: a UPI barcode, just above the left temple.

"What's with all the ruckus, Heller?" she asked. "I could hardly focus on making our Dude Day map, what with all the cheap chatter drifting upstairs."

She grabbed her nose and held. "Smells like burnt rubber. Did you fuck up the pizza?" When I didn't say anything, she laughed. "You did, didn't you? Burned at the stake, Joan of Arc dies for Wolfgang Puck." She laughed again. At me, of course. "Let's go drink some beers at the beach, get some greasy Eye-talian takeout. Whaddya say?"

"I say, SMD, H8er," I said in a quiet voice. "You're the one who's fucking everything up. Not me."

She shrugged. She was wearing my Diesel Lloyd jacket and a pair of my mom's Phillip Lim Seamed Leather Pants. Her legs were so bony the slacks hung wide at the thighs and bagged around her knees.

"Those pants cost like a thousand dollars, H8er. I'm so fucking glad you didn't come down while my mother was home. She would have killed me. Instead of just taking away my car keys."

"Fuck me! Tell me she didn't take the fucking keys to the van!" H8er roared, marching around the living room and stomping her feet. She had on a pair of my mother's *très* classic Acne embroidered mules. They were so tight I could see the outline of her toes poking up through the fuchsia silk. "Now how the fuck are we going to take down Hope Shore College on Monday? Call a cab?"

"Maybe my mom can drive us," I said in my most sarcastic tone. "We'll sit in the back seat with our duffle bag full of Grampy's firearms, and we'll chitchat with Mom about my failing grades, my rift with Trixie, my weight loss and crappy looking hairdo, my goddam headaches and my insomnia and my drinking and drugging and my fucking insanity. How's that sound?"

H8er stopped pacing and stared at me. Her face was icy. "Fuck you, Heller. Truth is, you're just too scared to go through with it. You're looking for any excuse to drop out. One small bump in the road and you bail. Total pussy behavior. Should have figured you'd cop out. Chickenshit nerd."

If I'd had a gun in my hand at that moment, I might have blown her fucking head off. How *dare* she accuse me of being a chicken? Yet another farm animal, one accorded so little respect.

Inside my concave belly, my gut burbled like a pot of boiling vinegar. Then the internal acid blew up. It fucking ignited and everything began to burn within me. All my organs caught fire, my hot bloodstream circulating, coursing through a low, blue, caustic flame. The internal, infernal, eternal flame.

Anger. It felt really good. For the first time in a long time, I felt like someone who could feel something. Something real. Something of my own.

"Look," I said between gritted teeth. My jaw melted down around each word as it left my blistering lips. "It's very simple. I'll convince Mom to let me drop her at work on Monday, like I'm going from there to school. Like I used to before I got the van. I'll come back here and we'll load up *her* car with our stuff. Then we'll head for the campus. No big change in plans, H8er. Nothing I can't handle."

She smirked at me, her mean mouth a rictus, the ball stud wriggling on her lip, trembling, as if to say, *Prove it, you big pussy.* I looked in her eyes. They were slate, black slate, reflecting nothing. Nothing at all.

She reached in her pocket (*my* fucking jacket pocket) and pulled out a slim silver flask. A very nice antique-looking flask I'd admired when it sat on a knickknack shelf in Trixie's dining alcove.

H8er held it up. "Absinthe. Goes great with Red Bull. Can really get your home fires burning."

"I don't need any revving up, thanks. I'm all ready to go."

My voice was calm. My hands were steady too as we went over the map H8er had drawn. We both acted cold as ice as we worked together to finalize our plan of attack.

But inside? I don't know about H8er, but inside I was on fire.

EPILOGUE

Last Day of Summer Classes, 2012

A S IT TURNED out, the plan did not go as expected. Life is like that. Ever notice?

On Monday, I drove Mom to work but did not go on to class like she expected me to. No, instead I returned home. Then H8er and I packed up the Land Rover with the way heavy duffle full of firearms, plus a bunch of ammo we'd ordered on the Internet. For some reason, I transferred the hand grenade into the glove compartment of Mom's car. Like we might need it? Or maybe for safe keeping. Duh. Whatever the reason, I deviated from the plan we'd so carefully studied.

So already I was veering off track. H8er didn't say anything, though. She seemed nervous, withdrawn. She kept slugging from Trixie's flask. Red Bull and absinthe, I guess. Or maybe just the absinthe. She chugalugged, I drove.

After I parked Mom's car in the student lot closest to Professor Dimitri's classroom, we took a few minutes to check out the route ahead of us. The sidewalks were almost empty, the campus nearly deserted. Monday morning, kids tucked away in their dorm rooms, sleeping off the remnants of weekend hangovers. A lot of profs don't expect or assign much during the last week of summer school anyway, but typically opt to let their students present lame oral reports. Some teachers provide tepid reviews for upcoming finals. More wasted time.

At that particular moment, the whole college experience seemed to me like a craptastic waste of money and time. But so did my life.

We waited for POPO to ride by, their muscular backs hunched over the slim handlebars of their twelve-speed bicycles. As usual, they passed us by, oblivious, all swoll and super jacked. The two meatheads were chatting and laughing together, like their job was a big joke.

"Like they could protect a school from girls like us," H8er sneered.

I didn't respond. My head spun and my blood felt hot. In fact, it broiled. It streamed fast and wild, crackling through my veins.

Somebody's done for, I thought.

On the way to work earlier in the morning, Mom had been in a weird mood. Sort of giddy and sad at the same time. She told me she thought maybe she was going to end things with Marc. I asked her why but she didn't really answer. I think she was kind of talking to herself when she said, "He already *has* a family. He doesn't want *ours*."

This made me feel all empty inside. Nobody wanted us. Nobody wanted me, of course. That was understandable. But nobody wanted Mom either. Poor Mom. She tried so hard to be loved.

When I stopped at Ocean for a red light, I leaned over and kind of hugged her. Pecked her soft cheek.

"Love you, Moms," I said.

She laughed, but not in a happy way. More like a distrustful, hesitant, almost scoffing way. "No fair. You're not going to get the van keys back from me *that* easily."

We smiled sadly at each other. Then the light changed and she said, "Go." Like I couldn't figure that out for myself.

"Let's go show dickweed who's boss," H8er said as we climbed out of the SUV.

We slid the bag from the back onto the hot asphalt. It weighed like a ton. The sun bounced off my neck and I felt sweat dripping down, pooling between my breasts. We stared at the duffle, then at each other.

"Tool up," H8er said.

Carefully following our Dude Day plan, we hoisted the heavy bag between us and carried it together, each hanging onto a nylon strap. If POPO rode by again and saw what we were lugging across the lot, they would smell a rat instantly. There was like nothing safe or sane that two students would bring to class in an Army Navy USMC Olive Drab Duffle bag. What we were up to was effing obvious.

But none of the kids we passed looked twice or said anything to us as we crossed the wide, freshly mown lawn and struggled up the stone steps of the humanities building. Everyone was sauntering around, backpacks fully loaded, staring at their smart phones or chatting on them, way deep in their own private worlds.

POPO did not return. Our timing was perfect.

We hustled into the building and up the double set of stairs, then grunted as we dropped the duffle onto the gray tile floor. I shrugged my shoulders around, loosening the muscles, and gave H8er a pained look that said, *Ouch, my arms are killing me.*

She frowned, all business, impatient. Like she was thinking, *You are such a wimp.*

Grabbing up the straps again, we dragged our bag down the hall to the Comp 100 classroom. The door was closed but you could hear Professor Dimitri's rumbling voice droning on and on. As we stood there getting our breath, he kept blathering. Right through the solid oak door came the deadening sound of hypnotic brainwash, the inane twaddle of professorial blahblahblah.

He was talking about the importance of developing a devotion to reading good literature. He was saying how if we didn't read, if we didn't read fine works of fiction and poetry and nonfiction, we'd never understand ourselves. We'd never understand life.

I had to laugh. I'd read all sorts of really great books but I had no clue who I was or what life was about. What life was supposed to be for. Literature was turning out to be just another religion. After all, I'd bowed at the altar of literature and where had it gotten me?

To here. Standing outside the door to my future. A future I couldn't even imagine, no matter how much mapping and talking and planning H8er and I had done.

My head pounding out some unrecognizable rhythm, I knelt down and unzipped the duffle. This was not part of the plan, but so what? I'd veered off track and now I was speeding through the woods toward an unknown destination. I reached in for whatever lay on top, tucking the heavy metal objects in my jacket pockets.

"The fuck you doing?" H8er whispered.

"Tooling up," I said softly, but by now I was out of control.

Hot salty sweat poured down my face, dripping into my eyes. I mean, who the fuck did he think he was? Why was he teaching a writing class to impressionable (albeit cynical and mostly unmotivated) young people? Nobody can *teach* you how to write. Writing is a personal act, an act of defiance. You just sit there and do it until it's done.

Marcus Dimitri was a useless prick. A total phony. A loser who made women suffer. He was bad for students, bad for the world. Why couldn't everyone see that?

I looked up at H8er from where I was still kneeling on the filthy floor, and she glared down at me. My heart drummed in my ears, and alongside it I could hear the steady beat of her pulse too. Like a little song. Our breathing was perfectly in sync. A duet.

Class had been in session for at least a half-hour. I was late. As usual. So fucking what?

H8er whispered, "On *three*, we go in."

I stood up, looked her in the eye, nodded.

She whispered, "One, two, *three*."

Professor Dimitri stood before the class, gesticulating wildly, saying nothing worthwhile. Getting off on the sound of his own voice. He didn't notice us at first because his back was to the class and he was pointing out something on the whiteboard. Some useless factoid that meant nothing.

Nothing at all.

We dragged the duffle bag into the room, up the aisle between neatly rowed desks, and across the front to the cheesy particle board podium. We stopped there.

It was hot, that was the first thing you would have noticed. And quiet, weird quiet like it is some Sunday mornings in church between songs. Like just after the choir finishes singing and the organ trails off and the notes ease up, soften, drift into mist, then drop away. The classroom smelled like Ivory soap, tropical fruit chewing gum, hazelnut coffee. The room had a lot of people in it but everyone was holding their breath, unmoving, in a kind of religious state of grace. The room itself was between breaths. Hot and still.

H8er reached into the duffle and pulled out the 12-gauge Savage-Springfield 67H pump-action shotgun. She looked badass in my rumpled Diesel Lloyd black leather jacket and my mom's skin-tightest black leggings. So tight they didn't bag off her popsicle-stick legs. I'd loaned her my made-to-order lizard skin cowboy boots with the stacked leather heels and the lemon wood pegs. She was a little wobbly on the Cuban heels, but she stood tall, her pale face serious as ever.

That was the thing about H8er. You could never tell when she was having a good time.

The silver ball stud on her upper lip bounced a little when she said quietly, "You gonna just stand there, pussy?" Which was, in a way, kind. Because she didn't want to embarrass me, with us standing up there like on display, in the front of the hushed classroom, everyone staring.

"Don't let's wait for the POPO to get here, *Heidi*," she added. Which wasn't so kind. She knew how much I hated to be called that.

I reached into the bag and pulled out a firearm. Another random choice. Lifted it up, held it firm like I knew what it took to shoot to kill. Aimed it at my teacher, my mother's lover, aimed it straight at his scruffy, middle-aged, full-of-his-own-bullshit head. The look on his face made me almost wet my pants. Part of me wanted to laugh, while the other part of me wanted to die.

The M1911A1 .45 caliber handgun was slip-sliding about in my sweaty palms. I could smell that distinctive oily metal odor, the cosmoline my grandfather used on all his guns. If she'd seen me my mom would have said, "For god's sake, Aimee, stand up straight!" Because I was tipped to the left from the Italian Beretta double-action semi-automatic pistol with 16-round double-stack magazines weighing down the front pocket of the Army-Navy Surplus fatigue jacket I'd taken from my grandfather's closet. Along with the hand grenade.

The grenade I'd left in the glove compartment of the Land Rover.

Shit! Fuck me. I was so out of it. If I didn't write myself a note, I forgot everything. I couldn't keep track anymore of what I wanted to do.

I hadn't even remembered to read *The Bell Jar*.

"These people are entering a world of pain, *your* world of pain," H8er said to me. "Show them who's not afraid to act like a man."

"Dude," I whispered. "You go first. Like, remember: this was *your* idea."

H8er tossed her head once or twice and a little clump of eggshell white bang hair bounced around her broad forehead. She lifted the shotgun and took aim. At nobody in particular, and everybody at once. Her finger tats gleamed with sweat. She must have been as scared as I was. But you would have been impressed by how pro she looked. Like Angelina Jolie in *Salt*.

Surprising myself, I suddenly sprang into action. It was like I'd been racing down the road and suddenly hit a tree. Boom, the path ended. Like that.

I mean, I just totally abandoned the plan we'd made to shoot up that class, then work our way around campus, shooting and shooting until we were killed by cops or we ran out of ammo. I just couldn't do it. It seemed so absurd. Really, was this how men thought? I wanted none of it.

So I bounced off the tree, and went rogue. Aimee H. Heller went rogue. Because I realized something in that fractured moment between breaths, between heartbeats, between the *do it* and the *it's done*. Something that changed me, changed my mind.

I can hardly describe to you what happened in that instant, it was so much like a dream. How the hot silent room kind of lifted me up, like I was in church and the organ had been playing and a song I really liked had just ended, and I was feeling clear headed, able to see through all the bullshit to some sort of wispy dust mote of truth. How I paused the movement of time right there, hovering, like on remote above a FOX news scene of yet another senseless school shooting horror. And how, at the same time, I saw myself in action. Like in the kind of dream where you are both observing and participating.

Like I was in a dream and watching myself in the dream. That's how I was able to actually see myself as I pointed the gun at my own head, first caressing my temple with it, then pressing the cold metal barrel to my lips. I smelled gun oil and sulfur. I accepted a hollow kiss. The dead bell rang in my head, where it had been tolling for months.

The dream continued. The dream lingered in a kind of time warp. And while it did, while it went on and on, I was thinking about how I wasn't really angry at my classmates. How it wasn't any of those kids' fault they were stuck in a stupid, useless writing class at one of the thousands of stupid, useless, overpriced colleges sucking up everyone's time and money and energy and innovative spirit and creative individuality. How all the kids staring at me, at us, their babyish faces rigid in fear, their young bodies frozen in their seats, all of them holding their breaths, but not hating me, or hating us, just scared and confused and wondering why, why me, her, us, them, they weren't the enemy, we weren't, I wasn't. Not me.

H8er.

Not me, H8er.

Before she pulled the trigger, I knew what she was going to say before she said it. "SMD, Aimee."

Suck my dick. Her favorite expression. Mine too. Our favorite thing to say to each other.

And the last thing Skitchen Sturter ever said to me. Because before she could squeeze the trigger, I took the gun from my crying mouth and turned it on her. I aimed it at the spot where, under her bleached bangs, a UPI code tattoo on her blue-white skin made fun of the world we lived in. *Ha, ha, this whole thing is a fucking joke*, H8er said with her unkempt body, her colorless eyes, her badass attitude, her trash talk and radical fem cant.

It wasn't, though. My life was not a joke.

I aimed and fired.

One shot. Close range.

Blew her fucking head off.

AFTERWORD

Last Day of the Writing Assignment

SO THAT'S IT. All she wrote. Done. Now you have it. What you said you wanted. My sorry-ass life story. The road badly traveled. Etcetera.

I know what you're thinking. I know all about your psychological assessments, your theories on adolescent rage, your clinical diagnoses of syndromes, disorders, this-isms and that-isms. But you're wrong. H8er *did* exist. *She was real.* And she was my BFF, she really was.

Until I killed her on the campus of Hope Shore College on the last day of summer school.

It really pisses me off how you've convinced my mom I made H8er up. Like she was just some ego extension, a fabricated idealization, a sick illusion created out of some wack neurosis I was suffering from. Like I had some kind of H8er Personality Disorder.

Ha. What a heap of bullshit. But now Mom believes you that H8er was just some adolescent phase I was going through, a deviant imaginary friend gone bad. All part of some months-long fugue state rich with delusions and hallucinations.

All possibly due to a serious case of Imposter Syndrome. Your current diagnosis.

Ridiculous. Imposter Syndrome is a weirdo scifi-ish mental disorder. It's crap. You really believe that I somehow believe I'm not deserving of my earned success? And that I'm so ego weak I'm dismissing all proof of the person I really am until I actually see myself as someone else?

Oh, come on! I can barely get my head around it, never mind pull it off!

Besides, if H8er was really me, the like worst part of me acting out some version of me, wouldn't *she* have shot *me* in the head? I mean if she and I were the same person, wouldn't she have known exactly what I was going to do?

Hellz yeah, you can bet H8er would've saved her own ass. She would've done whatever to stop me from killing her. So you'd be talking to H8er right now, you would've made *her* write about what happened, how it all went down.

Come on, Doc. I mean, your diagnosis is impressively complex, but it's off. Way off. Like so what if Mom found a bottle of Kitchen Starter under the sink? Some new cleaning product she bought last spring that does, I admit, sound a lot like Skitchen Sturter. But so what? Coincidences prove nothing.

You ask where H8er was from, who her parents were, where she lived, what schools she attended. When I say I don't know, none of that matters, we lived in the moment, we became something bigger than ourselves, you say nothing. You just get that knowing expression on your face. That shrink smirk. Like you're resting your case against me. Like I'm just your typical head case.

Can I say this? I get more out of talking to Siri than I get from my daily sessions with you.

Mom's even worse than you. It's like she wants me to have

like a brain tumor or epilepsy or something. She actually admitted that to me, that an organic reason for my behavior would be so much better for both of us. Any kind of frontal lobe dysfunction would please her, something foreign pressing on the hypothalamus, causing personality changes, acquired sociopathy, increased aggression. MRIs and CAT scans are, she says, the way to go. Surgery, drugs, anything to make me go backward in time to the docile, cooperative little Heidi I once was.

Mom says not to worry, though. That whatever the root cause, Uncle Moneybags will pay for my treatment.

Like I need a cure for who I am.

Mom wants so badly to believe I'm normal, that the whole mess is biological. Or a phase. A curable problem, a passing thing. Teens of single moms. Teens and alcohol. An adolescent reaction to the self-prescribed handfuls of Luvox. The Ambien, the Prozac. She so wants to believe that because I'm supposed to be such a reasonable and intelligent girl. Which maybe I used to be, but now I'm not. I can't tell you why. I told you already, I don't really understand myself. How did I become the kind of person you talk about when you want to feel better about yourself? Why did I think I was speaking for the era's most vengeful youth, why did I elect to express their unspoken existential rage? We're talking about unchecked aggression here, man.

Truth is, the resolution for this whole thing would be for me to stop being me. My unreliable self, right? But right now, the way I see it, I'm doomed to keep being me. Or at least to keep on impersonating the person who is supposed to be me. If I look at things your way.

BTW, you headshrinkers might want to stop diagnosing

every single person you shrink with some sort of stupidass disorder or disease. Some of us are crazy. Just plain loony. And some of us are not. Bad shit happens to us, and we cope. We fucking cope. Give us a little credit, will ya?

I mean, you keep saying you want me to get better. That my mom wants me to get better. And that Dads does too. Even though he has yet to show up here. (But hey, he *is* footing the gotta be massive bill for all this "treatment," so of course he wants a goddam cure.) You keep telling me how Bitsy is rooting for my improved mental health. Trixie too. My closest loved ones. So okay, I get all that.

But here's the thing: I think I *am* better. Better than how (or who) I used to be. BH. Before I met H8er. I was not myself back then. I was this sort of person, the girl Mom wanted me to be. The kind of superficial good girl the gender oppressive culture we live in was like forcing me to be. Heidi was doing all the right stuff and getting nothing for it. Nothing!

Don't you get it? I felt like nothing back then. I *felt* nothing.

And now? AH? After H8er? (May she rest in something other than peace, which would be totally unlike her.) Now I am myself. I am more myself than I've ever been in my whole fucking life.

And, hey: I really don't buy it that nobody died in that retard comp class at HSC. Are you kidding me? I was there! I saw what happened. Not what you keep telling me happened. I mean, it was just *not* the way you say it went down, with me just standing there by myself, looking like a freak in frumpy Army Navy Olive Drab, waving around Grampy's dusty old .45. Some silly Vietnam leftover he got at a yard sale. An old crap gun that wasn't even loaded. Pointing it at my own head, shooting blanks at nobody. At nothing.

Come on. I think not. That vanilla version of what occurred when Heller and H8er took on HSC? It just sounds like more of the bullshit you're using to trick me into not feeling so depressed about what I did to her. To my BFF. I know what you're up to, trying to give me a way to heal from the trauma. The trauma of killing my best friend.

Look: I feel horrible about the whole thing. I do. It was outrageous, abso-fuckin-lutely. Going on a shooting rampage, or even thinking about pulling one off, is really stupid. I'm embarrassed. What a fucked up idea. What a horrible thing to do. Dangerous, and so unnecessary.

So why don't we do something to stop people from turning on others like that? How come kids can grab military grade weapons, go out and take down classmates, family members, friends and strangers? It's like indulging oneself in a deadly shooting spree has become an American right. *Ring the dead bell, go ahead*, is what the culture seems to tell us.

Now, *that's* crazy.

So yeah, I'm like totally humiliated about what I did. But, like all the crummy self-help books say, it is what it is, what's done is done, WTF. H8er is gone from this fucked up world and I'm fucked. That's it. End of life story. Do with it what you will. Talking about it is not going to bring her back.

But you know what? I can accept that. I can live with knowing that truth, I guess. I mean, I *will* live. Okay?

So, like I said already, I'm done with my story. You can take it now, it's all yours. Go ahead and do whatever with this file, my written report. Take all these pages of whatever, of my sorry-ass life story, and just dump it. Burn it. Delete it. Poof. Gone. Or maybe you want to pore over it, show it to your headshrinker peers, your psych students. Study my psychopathology, the roots and the results. Write a paper, publish it in a peer reviewed journal.

Or you could email my story to Professor Dimitri. Tell him: Look, here's what Aimee Heller did on her summer vacation! Creative writing assignment extraordinaire.

Then maybe I wouldn't get an incomplete in that class after all.

Whatever. In the meantime, I'm going to try to write something else. I got nothing but time here. And notebook paper! Nothing but time and reams of lined notebook paper, available at cost in your crummy little lunatic asylum commissary. So maybe I'll write some fucking poetry. Creative nonfiction. How about a novel? One about a fucked up chick like me?

Hellz yeah.

So that's what *I'll* be doing. While *you* decide what to do with me. I'll be right here, hanging around all day in my no-brand cheap cotton scrubs, writing. Doing some *serious* writing. *Unassigned* writing.

How's that sound?

Crazy? *Crazy?*

SMD.

ADDENDUM

Oops, one more thing. I want you to have the poem and the essay I wrote last summer for Marcus Dimitri. I wrote these two papers, not H8er. I remember writing and editing them, handing them in. He thought the work sucked, but still, it *is* my own writing.

However, when I read both of them over again recently, after you told me I should reread all my old writing, it kind of didn't feel like the words were mine. It felt more like what I might have written when I was in the dream. The dream of being *that* person. *That* Aimee Heller. The girl who hooked up with H8er. The girl who launched herself out of Nerdvana and took off for the unknown. The girl who was changing, who was expressing her real self, who was becoming something more. The girl who was becoming someone else.

Whatever.

Thought you might like to add these papers to my file. Whatever you may be doing with that craptastic pile. So anyway, here they are. English Comp 100 Summer Assignments by Aimee Heller.

ADVICE TO POTENTIAL SUICIDES
BY AIMEE HELLER

Before you suck a hot tailpipe
or nestle the business end

of your father's dusty handgun
between your dentisty teeth

try gargling with gasoline
and smoking in a public park,
strapping yourself with C40
blowing the rest of us away.

Why go down easy like
a shot of Stoli
on a long dark night?
You can do better than that.

Start by not looking so close
at all the world's oozing zits.
Don't listen to the news anchor
morose about the body count,
another bloody war, mayhem, natural
disaster after disaster somewhere
you don't really care about.
Fuck that.

Think of your fellow man
and all the beautiful girls
the sorry slippery crust on each of us
our roped wrists, our wild laughter
the ticktick of our wind-up self-destruct.

Do not waste your precious death
for fuck's sake, friend

do not die

for yourself

alone.

ESSAY ON BIOLOGY AS DESTINY
BY AIMEE HELLER

According to recent research, all human behavior is the result of genetic programming and the resultant biological drives. We are our genes. We are not what we eat. We are not the result of our environment. So, if we are making bad choices, doing things the society considers immoral or illegal or even evil, it may be because that is how we are wired. In layman's terms, it's not our fault we fuck up.

Scientists think they know the exact areas of the brain responsible for empathy, aggression, and non-monogamous behavior. These physiological areas are influenced by our hormones and neurochemicals. So our bodies create the bathwater and we are soaking in it. Sometimes it's too hot, sometimes it's too cold. And sometimes it's just perfect.

The descendants of primates and primitives, we all have the capacity for committing atrocities. So why don't more of us commit them? And why is it mostly men who do? War, terrorism, spree and serial killing? Mostly male perpetrators. Imelda Marcos shopped for shoes while her husband committed the most heinous crimes. Where was Bernie Madoff's wife? At the local Gucci store. Women tend to turn away, while their evil partners do the bloody work. Why is this? Is it because females are inherently more moral than males?

Maybe it's because our brains are different.

Biologist Simon Baron-Cohen has looked at empathy and the genes that contribute to this trait. He found that men tend to have lower levels of empathy than women and surmised that this may be due to hormones. Guys lack the hormones that boost empathy. And then there's their prenatal hormone levels, the boost of testosterone in boy fetuses that contributes to the masculization of the brain. So maybe guys can't help it, not with all that circulating testosterone they're born with.

Some warrior cultures have genes that allow for more of certain neurotransmitters to remain in circulation in the brain, resulting in higher levels of aggression. This, too, is a masculine trait. A genetic trait. A biological predisposition.

Robert Hare has studied psychopaths and he estimates that they make up one percent of the population. His research has concluded that they lack normal limbic system responses, and that they may have dysfunctional amygdalae. This biological deviance is more common in males. More males than females have psychopathic brains.

It sure looks like guys are the ones with the hormones, the genes, and the brains that tend toward antisocial, violent, and evil behavior.

Personally, I think we all have some good and some evil in us. This is my own belief based on what I've read in my psychology and English literature classes, as well as what I've observed. Girls can certainly act out and get violent just as easily as boys do, but the tendency to do so may be less strong due to conditioning. Girls in this culture are repressed. Even though the previous era of feminist enlightenment and current women's rights have provided girls my age with more opportunities and less sexual bias, society still tells us how to behave. So boys are the ones who get in fights and girls are just mean with their words. Boys shoot off guns and girls cut themselves. Boys go on rampages and girls take overdoses.

To be honest, I'm not sure I buy all that biological determination stuff. It makes sense, yeah, but it feels a lot like old-fashioned sexism. Like girls aren't capable of despicable acts because they've got bodies designed primarily to give birth. I don't buy it. I don't believe that biology is our destiny and that's all we got.

But I will say, our biology sure seems to direct our life choices. And I, for one, see this as totally uninspiring. I aim to make my own choices in life. Biology can SMD.

ACKNOWLEDGEMENTS

To narrow down the list of fictional influences
that led to the creation of this book is impossible. Every
book I've ever read about girls, both good girls and the not so
well behaved, has contributed to the creating of this one. But
I must admit it was Jim Shepard's exceptional novel *Project
X* that inspired me to write the female version of what might
happen when two kids decide to shoot up a school. I also
loved DBG Pierre's wildly wonderful *Vernon God Little*. I
loved it so much I wanted to see a girl do some of the same
things Pierre's protagonist did in that novel. And truth be
told, Chuck Palahniuk's awesome *Fight Club* had an impact
on this story. But that book infiltrates all of my writing on
some level. Subatomic, maybe. That book is in my blood. Like
a virus that just won't go away.

I owe much to my stalwart and insightful writing group,
Ink Well of South Florida, especially Brenda Ferber, an
amazing writer and one-woman cheerleading team. And to my
writing partner, Athena Sasso. I am also grateful to Writers
in Paradise, and to Dennis Lehane, the bestselling novelist
behind that influential annual event. You want to learn how
to write good fiction? Attend the next Writers in Paradise.

Many thanks to Jen, Chris, and everyone at Salt Publishing
for taking a chance on this book. Best literary press ever! And
to Linda Bennett, editor extraordinaire with always a kind
word for tormented writers.

Also, a big hug to my first reader/best reader, Mel Goss. Thanks, Mel, for being so enthusiastic about this story. Hugs to my writer husband, who knows just how much it hurts to keep on keeping on.

Note: The chapter Crapesthetic was published as short fiction in an altered form in the July 2014 issue of *Big Pulp*.

AUTHOR'S NOTE

THIS BOOK IS fictional and any resemblance of the characters to persons living or dead is entirely coincidental. The story is not meant to inspire actions or suggest that violence is a viable or cool option for young women. It isn't. It's the worst choice imaginable. As a work of fiction, the literary perceptions and insights are based on experience, but all the names, characters, places, and incidents are products of the author's highly creative (and kind of scary wild) imagination. Except for the brand names. Believe it or not, almost all the brands in the book are real. However, use of these particular brands is not meant to imply a correlation with insanity, greed, bad behavior or psychopathology. Obviously. Duh.

NEW BOOKS FROM SALT

XAN BROOKS
The Clocks in This House All Tell Different Times
(978-1-78463-093-5)

RON BUTLIN
Billionaires' Banquet (978-1-78463-100-0)

MICKEY J CORRIGAN
Project XX (978-1-78463-097-3)

MARIE GAMESON
The Giddy Career of Mr Gadd (deceased) (978-1-78463-118-5)

LESLEY GLAISTER
The Squeeze (978-1-78463-116-1)

NAOMI HAMILL
How To Be a Kosovan Bride (978-1-78463-095-9)

CHRISTINA JAMES
Fair of Face (978-1-78463-108-6)

SIMON KINCH
Two Sketches of Disjointed Happiness (978-1-78463-110-9)

This book has been typeset by
SALT PUBLISHING LIMITED
using Neacademia, a font designed by Sergei Egorov
for the Rosetta Type Foundry in the Czech Republic.
It is manufactured using Creamy 70gsm, a Forest
Stewardship Council™ certified paper from Stora Enso's
Anjala Mill in Finland. It was printed and bound by
Clays Limited in Bungay, Suffolk, Great Britain.

LONDON
GREAT BRITAIN
MMXVII